The House of Robots Series by James Patterson

House of Robots
House of Robots: Robots Go Wild!
House of Robots: Robot Revolution

The Daniel X Series by James Patterson

The Dangerous Days of Daniel X
Daniel X: Watch the Skies
Daniel X: Demons and Druids
Daniel X: Game Over
Daniel X: Armageddon
Daniel X: Lights Out

Other Illustrated Novels and Stories

Max Einstein: The Genius Experiment
Not So Normal Norbert
Unbelievably Boring Bart
Pottymouth and Stoopid
Laugh Out Loud
Jacky Ha-Ha
Jacky Ha-Ha: My Life Is a Joke
Public School Superhero
Word of Mouse
Give Please a Chance
Give Thank You a Try
Big Words for Little Geniuses
Cuddly Critters for Little Geniuses
The Candies Save Christmas

For exclusives, trailers, and other information, visit
jimmypatterson.org.

Hi, I'm JIMMY!

Like me, you probably noticed the world is run by adults.
But ask yourself: Who would do the best job
of making books that *kids* will love?
Yeah. **Kids!**

So that's how the idea of JIMMY books came to life.
We want every JIMMY book to be so good
that when you're finished, you'll say,

"PLEASE GIVE ME ANOTHER BOOK!"

Give this one a try and see if you agree.
(If not, you're probably an adult!)

JIMMY PATTERSON BOOKS
for Young Readers

James Patterson Presents

The Middle School Series by James Patterson

The I Funny Series by James Patterson

The Treasure Hunters Series by James Patterson

POTTYMOUTH AND STOOPID

POTTYMOUTH AND STOOPID

JAMES PATTERSON
AND CHRIS GRABENSTEIN

ILLUSTRATED BY STEPHEN GILPIN

Jimmy Patterson Books
LITTLE, BROWN AND COMPANY
New York Boston London

Copyright © 2017 by James Patterson
Illustrations by Stephen Gilpin
Excerpt from *Max Einstein: The Genius Experiment* copyright © 2018 by James Patterson
Excerpt illustrations by Beverly Johnson

JIMMY Patterson Books / Little, Brown and Company
Hachette Book Group
1290 Avenue of the Americas, New York, NY 10104
jimmypatterson.org

First paperback edition: March 2019
Originally published in hardcover by JIMMY Patterson Books / Little, Brown and Company, June 2017

JIMMY Patterson Books is an imprint of Little, Brown and Company, a division of Hachette Book Group, Inc. The Little, Brown name and logo are trademarks of Hachette Book Group, Inc. The JIMMY Patterson Books® name and logo are trademarks of JBP Business, LLC.

The publisher is not responsible for websites (or their content) that are not owned by the publisher.

The Hachette Speakers Bureau provides a wide range of authors for speaking events. To find out more, go to hachettespeakersbureau.com or call (866) 376-6591.

Library of Congress Cataloging-in-Publication Data

Names: Patterson, James. | Grabenstein, Chris, author. |
    Gilpin, Stephen, illustrator.
Title: Pottymouth & Stoopid / James Patterson and Chris Grabenstein ;
    illustrated by Stephen Gilpin.
Other titles: Pottymouth and Stoopid
Description: First edition. | New York : Little, Brown and Company, 2017. |
    "Jimmy Patterson Books." | Summary: Two bullied underdogs finally win the day
    when their troubles inspire a hit TV show"— Provided by publisher.
Identifiers: LCCN 2016002100 | ISBN 978-0-316-34963-5 (hc) | 978-0-316-51498-9 (pb)
Subjects: | CYAC: Best friends—Fiction. | Friendship—Fiction. |
    Behavior—Fiction. | Fame—Fiction. | Television programs—Fiction. |
    Middle schools—Fiction. | Schools—Fiction.
Classification: LCC PZ7.P27653 Po 2016 | DDC [Fic]—dc23 LC record available at
https://lccn.loc.gov/2016002100

10 9 8 7 6 5 4 3 2 1

LSC-C

Printed in the United States of America

To Michael Thompson, PhD, and Dan Kindlon, PhD,
coauthors of Raising Cain, *who first got me thinking*
about the insidious nature and dire consequences
of bullying boys

Prologue

Can We Have Your Attention, Please?
Didn't Think So

Welcome to the big speech where the whole school has to listen to me, "Stoopid," and my best bud since forever, "Pottymouth."

Actually, they don't let Pottymouth talk too much in public. Especially not with a microphone.

So, looks like you're stuck with just me.

And I bet you're wondering why.

Okay. Everybody here already knows us, right? We're Pottymouth and Stoopid, thanks to all of you. Those have been our nicknames since you gave them to us, like, forever ago. We're the class clowns.

No, wait. We're the class *jokes*.

Wow. We actually look like us and everything.

Well, today you'll hear our real, true story. And we get to tell it our way. We might let some other people chime in, but it's mostly going to be us because, come on, this is *our* story.

I'll apologize to your butts now, because they'll be pretty sore from sitting here by the time I'm done. See, I'm going to start at the very beginning. Way, way back in the olden days when we were just little David and mini-Michael and our biggest problems were dirty diapers.

Now, everybody pay attention. Even you teachers.

You might actually learn some things you didn't know about Pottymouth and Stoopid.

You might also learn that some of the things you thought you knew are totally and completely wrong.

PART ONE

Before We Became Famous

Mrs. L. Rabinowitz

**Pottymouth and Stoopid's
Preschool Teacher**

Oh, I remember Michael and David.

They were both so squirrelly.

Natural-born troublemakers.

You know how one rotten apple can spoil the whole barrel?

Try dealing with *two!*

Stoopid: The Origin Story

Okay, the first time I met Michael Littlefield was in the second week of preschool. I remember that, even back when we were just four years old, Michael could crack me up like nobody else. What can I say? He always had a way with words.

"Poop!" he said when I showed him the picture of blue squiggles I'd dribbled off the tip of my brush. "Blue poop."

That, of course, made me giggle. So I told him my name. "I'm David!"

"I'm Michael!"

We toddled back to the art-supplies cabinet because I knew there was still some blue paint left in the jar.

Our teacher, Mrs. Rabinowitz—who always had a headache—wasn't really watching us or paying much attention to anybody. Except her favorite kid, Kaya Kennecky, a girl who came to pre-K every morning in matchy-matchy outfits complete with a matching bow in her curly blond hair.

While Michael and I played with the paint, Kaya sat in Mrs. Rabinowitz's lap reading a picture book about a caterpillar who was ridiculously hungry. So Mrs. Rabinowitz didn't see me dribble paint all over Michael's shoes.

"Poop!" he said. "Blue poop!"

Yes, back then, Michael liked to talk about pee and poop and poopypants because, let's be honest here, when you're a kid in preschool, bodily functions are hysterical. Underpants too.

"Booger butt!" Michael blurted and I cracked up.

Still laughing, I put the blue paint jar back on the shelf. And, yes, I forgot to screw the lid back on.

"Want red?" I asked.

He stuck out his left foot. "Red poop!"

I grabbed the jar of red paint. But the lid wouldn't come off. It was kind of stuck to the dried-out paint. It was like trying to twist open an antique tube of toothpaste.

I'd seen my dad, who was still living with us at the time, bang pickle jars on the kitchen counter when he couldn't twist their lids open. So that's what I did. I banged the jar of red paint against the wobbly steel shelf inside the art-supplies cabinet. I banged it so hard, the lid cracked and flew off. Paint sloshed out all over the place. And all that banging knocked the open blue jar off the shelf too.

Every inch of my hands, face, and clothes that wasn't already speckled red was splattered blue. Michael's clothes were a mess too. But his shoes—squiggly blue and splotchy red—looked incredibly cool (to a four-year-old, anyway).

"Awesomesauce!" we both yelled.

Kaya heard us and saw the disaster we'd made. "Mrs. Rabinowitz!" she hollered. "That stupid boy did something stupid!"

Since I was still holding the jar of red paint in my hand, it was pretty obvious who she was calling stupid.

"You're so stupid, David," Kaya cried. "You're just a stupid-head. You're so stupid, stupid, stupid! You're the stupidest boy ever!"

Everybody in the class started laughing and

pointing and chanting "Stoopid," drawing out the *oo* sound. Mrs. Rabinowitz was busy trying to clean up my mess so she didn't have time to remind everybody that name-calling was strictly against the rules.

I, of course, wasn't laughing. What I did with the paint jars might've been dumb, but that didn't automatically make me *stupid*.

Except it kind of did. It made me Stoopid. With a capital *S*.

Well, to everybody except my paint-spattered partner in crime.

"You're not stupid, David," Michael told me. "You're my best friend!"

If David is stupid, then I must be stupider because I like him.

Stoopid:
The Legend Continues

Things didn't get much better when Michael and I moved up to kindergarten.

Okay, they got way worse. I still did some dumb stuff, like calling the graham crackers we had for snack "grand crappers."

I remember the teacher, Ms. Stone, asked me if I could spell my mom's name. I said, "Yes! M-O-M."

Kaya Kennecky was still in our class. "That boy's name is Stoopid," she told Ms. Stone. "A lot of boys are dumb, but he's the stupidest boy in the whole world!"

"We don't use that word in this class, Kaya," said Ms. Stone.

"Well, what do you call stupid people, then? Idiots?"

I did some other dumb stuff that didn't help my kindergarten reputation any. Once, when I needed Ms. Stone's help tying my shoe, she asked me, "What's the magic word?" I said, "Abracadabra."

When she asked me to try again, I said, "Shazam?"

But does that make me Stoopid or just, you know, a normal kid?

Actually, for a little while, I thought my teacher, Ms. Stone, might be sort of stupid herself. She kept asking us to name all the colors in the crayon box. Didn't she know what they were called? The names were printed right on the wrappers.

In kindergarten, I also had a lot of what they called "excess energy."

You know how some kids act at a birthday party after they eat ice cream and cake and chug soda to wash down all the jelly beans and Laffy Taffy in the goodie bags? That was me on a normal day. I just don't like sitting still, and, unfortunately, a lot of school involves sitting and not fidgeting.

I remember this time when Ms. Stone wanted us to sit on the alphabet rug on the letters of our first names.

I started on the *D*, got bored, scooted over to the *A*, then rolled over to the *V*. Ms. Stone told me she'd meant "just the first letter of your first name."

"Then he should sit on the *S*," said guess who. "For Stoopid!"

She got sent to the corner for that one, which only made her more determined to call me Stoopid every chance she got—just not in front of Ms. Stone.

I don't know why Kaya hated me so much even back then, but I've got to hand it to her: she tried super-hard to convince all the other kids to call me that, and it worked. After kindergarten, the name just sort of stuck.

Kaya Kennecky

Pottymouth and Stoopid's Classmate

Um, sorry, I don't mean to interrupt this flashback sequence or anything, but I have to butt in and let people know that Stoopid has always been totally and completely stupid!

I've known that dummy since pre-K when he used to go backward down the slide and do these crazy flips that could've hurt somebody.

In first grade, he wouldn't color things right. He made the sky green and the grass red.

One time, he tried to eat an eraser because it looked like a mini-marshmallow.

Duuuuuumb!

So how come Stoopid gets to have his own stupid assembly with his demented friend Pottymouth? He's totally making me sound bad with all of his lies about how I'm the one who started calling him Stoopid. I mean, even if I was, I obviously had a good reason for it!

I should have my own assembly with my friend Tiffany. We could show everyone our cheers and then twirl batons and do cartwheels. Even if we just sat there and read the dictionary out loud, it would be way better than this lame-o assembly about Pottymouth and Stoopid's life story!

I hope I'm not coming across as mean, because I'm not. I'm just being honest.

:)

3

There Are Worse Things in Life

After kindergarten that day, my mom picked me up in our clunker of a car, which I guess was further proof to my classmates (especially the ones like Kaya) that I was Stoopid!

The car was a piece of junk, but it wasn't our fault. My mom divorced my dad the summer before I started kindergarten, and he wasn't big on paying child support. (I'm sorry, but that's the truth, Ex-Dad, and I just told everybody I'd be giving them the real, true story of Pottymouth and Stoopid, so I can't cut you any slack.)

He was even worse at paying *car* support.

"Whaddaya need a new car for?" he'd say to my mom.

"To drive to the two more jobs I had to get so I can earn enough money to pay for everything *you're* not paying for."

"Well, I can't afford a new car for myself so I'm definitely not buying one for *you*."

"If you won't buy it for me, do it for your son."

"What? Why does David need a car? He's only four."

"Five."

"Whatever. He's not getting a new car. He doesn't even have a driver's license."

"You're crazy, Anthony; you know that, right?"

"Of course I'm crazy. I married *you*, didn't I?"

(Hey, if you think my mom and ex-dad can bicker, wait till you meet Michael's foster parents. My folks are amateurs compared to them.)

As you can tell, things were kind of ugly back then between my mom and dad. I guess that's what happens right after you get divorced. They've been split up for seven years now, so things have mellowed a little.

I'm only five, but even I know that arguing like this would be called bad parenting.

Well, they *had* mellowed until, you know, the big surprise.

More about that later.

Anyway, I told Mom what happened at school. "All the kids are calling me Stoopid!"

"Sorry, honey-bunny," Mom said with a sigh. "But it's not the end of the world. Trust me, there are worse things in life than being called stupid by some dumb clucks in kindergarten."

I sat there and thought about that for a long minute.

Finally I asked, "Like what?"

Mom thought about it for only half a second. "Not being able to go to school because the car won't start."

Well, if you'd asked me right then and there, having to stay home from school for any reason sounded pretty great.

Pottymouth:
The Origin Story

Let's jump ahead to third grade.

Michael and I were still in the same class. One day, we had a substitute teacher named Mr. Chaffapopoulos. I remember his name because Michael said it sounded like Mr. Snuffleupagus from *Sesame Street*.

Anyway, we were doing math. I was up at the whiteboard.

"Diana's mom gave her sixty-five dollars to go shopping," said Mr. Chaffapopoulos as I fidgeted with the dry-erase marker in my hand. "She bought a sweater for twenty-nine dollars, a T-shirt for twelve dollars, and a pair of shoes for fifteen. How much money does Diana have left?"

I knew it was a multistep problem.

I knew because those were, and still are, my least favorite kind.

The first thing I needed to do was write down all those numbers. I remembered the girl in the word problem started with sixty-five dollars. So I wrote 65 and a minus sign on the whiteboard.

"Um, how much was the sweater?" I asked.

"Twenty-nine dollars."

I wrote 29 after the first minus sign and added another minus sign.

"How much was the T-shirt?"

"Twwwwelllve. Dolllllaaarrrs."

He said it real slow, like he thought that was the only speed my brain would understand. Kids started snickering.

As I wrote 12, I started muttering to myself. "Short attention span, lack of focus, needs to develop better listening skills... "

It was all the stuff my teachers had written on

my report cards in first and second grade.

I didn't want to ask what the girl in the word problem bought next because the sub would definitely make fun of me again. He didn't know anything about my short attention span because he was a short-timer himself. So I wrote another minus sign and just made up the final number: 7.50.

"Excuse me," said Mr. Chaffapopoulos. "What exactly did Diane buy for seven dollars and fifty cents?"

The classroom tittered in anticipation of my dumb answer.

"Um, dog food?"

The whole classroom burst into a big laugh. After the laughter peaked, the whole classroom started chanting: "Stupid, stupid, David is stupid!"

Mr. Chaffapopoulos tried to make them be quiet. It didn't work. Like I said, he was a sub.

This was when Michael exploded.

"Rrrrrggghhh, *hicklesnicklepox!* David isn't stupid, you flufferknuckles! He's my friend, so stick your grizzlenoogies in your boomboolies and leave him alone."

"Huh?" said Kaya, who was still in our class (we just couldn't shake her).

"Sit down, Michael," said Mr. Chaffapopoulos in his most menacing voice. "Sit down this instant!"

"Ah, sludgepuggle, you flufferknuckle! Sludgepuggle, sludgepuggle, sludgepuggle!"

Mr. Chaffapopoulos gasped in horror. "Enough! I'm writing a note to your parents, Michael." He started scribbling something on a small pink pad. "They need to teach you what words are appropriate to use in school and what words are not. Then they need to wash your mouth out with hand sanitizer, Mr. Pottymouth!"

"Ha!" laughed a bunch of kids. "He's Mr. Pottymouth!"

Yep. This was the day Michael became known as Mr. Pottymouth, which, in less than a day, was shortened to Pottymouth.

5

Michael's House of Pottymouthing

After school that day, we went to Michael's house. Mr. Chaffapopoulos had demanded that Michael have both his parents sign his pink note to prove that they had read and understood what was written on it.

Slight problem. Michael didn't really have parents. He had foster parents. That meant he lived in their house and the state paid them to take care of him. He's never met his real parents. Before foster care, he lived in orphanages.

He and I have both been wondering if his real

folks would like to meet him now that he's kind of famous.

Well, if they do show up, Michael told me he's going to look at them and say, "Stick your grizzlenoogies in your boomboolies, you lazy flufferknuckles."

Where was I? Oh, right. Third grade. (See what I mean about my short attention span? There are gnats that remember stuff better than me.)

We walked into Michael's foster home with the pink slip. Mr. and Mrs. Brawley were both out of work back then. (Come to think of it, they're still both out of work.) The only money coming into the house was the cash the state paid them to take care of Michael and five other foster kids.

I'm not an expert on this stuff, but that day in the Brawley house, I think I figured out where Michael picked up his colorful language skills: the same place most pottymouths do. Home.

Since his foster parents didn't have jobs, they spent pretty much all of their time watching TV and fighting.

"Give me the @#$&% remote control, Shirley,"

his foster dad was saying when we walked into the living room.

"Why should I give you the @#$&% remote, you &@%#!?" answered his foster mom.

"Who are you calling a &@%#, you &@%#!"

I actually thought Michael's words—*hickle-snicklepox, flufferknuckle, grizzlenoogies, boomboolies,* and *sludgepuggle*—were way more inventive than the words his foster parents used. They were just saying the same old words all grown-ups say when things don't go their way or they hit themselves on the thumb with a hammer.

"I want to watch @^&*# Judge Judy," said Michael's foster dad.

"Because you're a !#&@*," said his foster mom. "Everyone knows Judge Joe Brown is a better @#$%+ judge than that $#@^& Judge Judy!"

While they were fighting, Michael saw his chance.

"Um, you guys?" He put the pink slip of paper on the tray table between them. "I need you both to sign this snifflefliggly thing."

"What the @^&*# is it?" asked his foster father.

"A &@%#! slip of pink paper," said his foster mother. "Are you &@%#$ blind?"

Furious, Mr. Brawley glared at his wife and signed the piece of paper without even looking at it. "At least I know how to spell my $#@%^ name!"

"I know how to spell your %$#@& name too: L-O-S-E-R!" Mrs. Brawley said as she glared back. Eyes locked, they were in a classic stare-off. Neither one wanted to be the first to blink or look away.

Yep. She signed the pink slip just like his foster father had—without even glancing at it.

"Thanks," said Michael, swiping the signed paper off the tray table while his foster parents kept up their stare-off.

We spent the rest of the afternoon up in the tree house that some of the older foster kids had built. Michael sat in one corner fuming. I sat in the other and nodded because I knew what he was thinking, the same way Michael usually knows what I'm thinking.

"I don't care what Mr. Snuffleupagus says," said Michael. "I'm not a pottymouth."

"I know. I was thinking the same thing."

"Hicklesnicklepox."

"Yeah. I was thinking that too."

PROFESSOR H. R. TWEED, PhD

Language Expert

What Michael Littlefield has done is nothing short of extraordinary.

He has created his own words. His own secret language, if you will.

The fact that nobody else understands what he is saying (except, perhaps, his best friend, David) does not make his linguistic accomplishment any less extraordinary.

Michael's achievement reminds me of Warlpiri

rampaku, or Light Warlpiri, a fascinating new language spoken only by people under the age of thirty-five in Lajamanu, an isolated village of about seven hundred indigenous citizens in Australia's Northern Territory.

When I informed Michael that I hoped to write a scholarly article about him and his extraordinary new language, he called me a flufferknuckle.

I must conduct further research on what that means.

A Few Years Later... and Nothing Much Has Changed

Four years later, Michael and I turned twelve. We'd also been Pottymouth and Stoopid for nearly half our lives. Most of the kids in our seventh-grade class didn't even know our real names. During roll call, when the teacher said, "Michael?" some kid would always shout, "She means Pottymouth!" Same thing when she said, "David?" Someone would yell, "Just call him Stoopid!" Everyone else would laugh. It was hysterical.

Unless, of course, you happened to be Michael or me.

So I don't want to give you a blow-by-blow account of grades four through seven. Why should we make *you* suffer through it all too? But I'll give you a few of the highlights.

Like the time we had to take an IQ test.

In case you don't know, an IQ is a person's intelligence quotient. This test was supposed to measure how smart we were. Most people have IQs of somewhere between 85 and 115. Only 5 percent score above 125.

Everybody was guessing I'd score somewhere in the 50s.

I remember one of the questions: "What are clothes made of?" You were given a bunch of answers to choose from: *cloth, paper, wood, glass,* and *I don't know.* When I saw that question, I seriously started wondering about the intelligence quotients of the people who wrote the IQ test. Come on, the answer's right in the question! If clothes were made out of glass, they'd be called glasses.

They never told us our IQ scores. I didn't want to know. I was probably afraid to find out that I really *was* stupid.

Another highlight? Hanging out in Michael's tree house reading comic books instead of going to school. Neither one of us ever won a perfect-attendance certificate. In fact, we both hated school so much, I think we would've won the district-wide competition for most unexcused absences if, you know, they had an award for that.

We weren't too good with after-school activities either. They kicked me out of the robotics club when I said I wanted to meet C-3PO. The chess club gave us both the boot because Michael liked to make up funny voices for the king and queen pieces: "Off with their heads!" "Yes, dear."

Even trick-or-treating on Halloween was a nightmare. One year, Michael and I made an extremely unfortunate choice of costume.

Okay, I admit it was truly stupid.

What can I say? We both loved the movie. The first one. Not the sequel.

On the plus side, for one night at the end of October, nobody called us Pottymouth and Stoopid.

We were just Dumb and Dumber.

7

Air Stoopid

One thing I might've actually been pretty good at if I'd ever gotten the chance?

Sports.

All that fidgety, squirrelly energy I had back in kindergarten was still with me in seventh grade. But now that I was older, I could run and jump like crazy.

Once, Coach Ball, the phys-ed teacher, told us to run around the gym four times.

Everybody else did four laps, but I did about eighty.

You see, I thought Coach Ball had said "for the whole time," so I kept going until the bell rang.

I might've been pretty good at basketball, but in gym class, nobody ever picked Pottymouth or me when choosing up sides. We always spent our gym time "riding the pine." That meant we sat on the bench and watched other guys play.

We got so bored, Michael would slide his butt across the bleachers so it would make squeaky noises that sounded like all sorts of different farts, which he gave all sorts of different names to.

The Chinese Firecracker. The Power Saw. The Quiver. And, of course, the Rusty Gate.

Michael always cracked me up. He still does.

After school (and on those days when we skipped school), we played our own brand of basketball at his house because, years ago, one of his foster brothers had put up a hoop over the garage door. The net was long gone, but all we needed was a hoop and a backboard.

We'd make up imaginary games and narrate them. I did most of the dribbling and shooting. Michael did most of the commentary.

"David for three from the top of the key!" he'd say in his best courtside-TV voice. "He shoots! Frizzlenitts...no good. Off the front of the rim... wait...now David grabs his own rebound. He slam-dunks it for an easy two and picks up a foul from that hoopiedoodle hicklesnicklepox who just elbowed him! David's heading to the line. It's up. It's good. Sludgepuggle, sludgepuggle, sludgepuggle!"

We played so much one-on-one against each other, so many games of HORSE, we got kind of bored with regular basketball and invented our own brand-new kind.

Michael called it Skateboardball. Because, if you haven't already guessed, it combined skateboarding with b-ball.

You scored extra points if you added tricks—maybe a fakie or a goofy-foot—when you shot. Pretty soon, I could do a kick-flip, spring off the board, and dunk. It was like I had springs in my legs. It was totally awesome.

You Can Look It Up in Our Anna Britannica

Somehow, Michael and I convinced ourselves that we were so good at Skateboardball, we should try out for the middle-school basketball team.

"Who did this?" said Coach Ball when he saw our names on the sign-up sheet. "Who thinks this is funny?"

Not exactly a vote of confidence for us.

"Um, we signed up ourselves," said Michael bravely.

Coach Ball squinted. "You're the kid who makes up all those weird words, right?"

"Snifflepiggle. Sometimes."

"Sorry, kid. No way am I risking you trash-talking the other team. Pottymouthing is considered unsportsmanlike conduct. You'd pick up so many technical fouls, we'd have to forfeit every game. Try the gardening club instead."

So much for our pro-basketball ambitions.

The only good thing that came from basketball

tryouts was meeting Anna Brittoni, the unofficial scorekeeper for the team.

By *unofficial*, I mean she liked basketball so much she asked Santa Claus to bring her a scorebook every Christmas so she could sit by herself at the games, eat stadium popcorn, and make little marks in her book.

Anyway, after Coach Ball refused to let us try out for the team, Michael and I trudged toward the exit, feeling dejected. There was only one person sitting in the bleachers on that side of the gym—Anna.

"I heard what Coach Ball just told you," she said, her cheeks turning bright pink because (we found out later) she was extremely shy. "He was wrong. I mean, about the technical fouls. In the middle-school league, once you earn two technical fouls for unsportsmanlike conduct, you're automatically ejected from the game. So your 'pottymouthing' would cost the team, at most, four points per game. Ergo," she said.

"I think there's some other reason Coach Ball doesn't want you on his team," said Anna.

"We know," I told her. "In case you haven't heard, Michael's Pottymouth and I'm Stoopid."

"Oh. I've heard about you two. I'm Anna Brittoni."

We were all about to shake hands when Kaya Kennecky and her friend Tiffany Blurke strutted across the shiny gym floor.

"Why, look, Tiffany. It's Pottymouth, Stoopid, and Anna Britannica."

Anna's cheeks turned pink again.

"Um, are you from Britain?" Michael asked.

Anna shook her head. "*Britannica* is the name of an encyclopedia."

"Like Encyclopedia Brown?" I asked.

Anna nodded. "Kaya and her friends call me Anna Britannica because being smart isn't exactly considered cool at this school."

"A lot of stuff is considered uncool around here," I said. "Being smart. Being different."

"Or," added Michael, "just being me and David."

COACH ED BALL

Gym Teacher

Guess who's feeling stupid now?

We've lost every basketball game this season. The popcorn guy gets more cheers than my first-string team.

The other day, I found this DVD in my mailbox. Anna Brittoni sent it to me. It was a video of that kid David dunking!

Sure, he did his dunk off a skateboard, but the kid's got game. I could've used him.

No, I *needed* him.

So call me Stoopid.

All the other coaches sure do.

Grandpas Are
Always Right

Did I mention that Michael and I live on the same street? Our houses are kind of simple, one-story deals. There are no jumbo-size McMansions on our block.

My mom and I moved to this house right after my ex-dad dumped us. At the time, he thought he was going to become a famous author. The next Ernest Hemingway. Hemingway's the guy who wrote the book about the old man who goes fishing in the sea, which, you know, is a good place to find fish.

At the time, Ex-Dad wasn't writing books about fish or old men. He was writing TV commercials about used cars for a local advertising agency called Finkle, Fry, and Farnsworth. They did some totally annoying spots for Big Bob's Auto Barn, the ones where Big Bob's big head floats around his car lot.

I'm Big Bob, and nobody beats my prices. I mean no body. Get it? That's why I'm always a-head of the competition.

Yeah. My ex-dad came up with that one.

My mom had three different jobs. Weekday mornings, she waitressed at an IHOP. After that, she rang a register and restocked shelves at

Walmart. Weekends, she cleaned doctors' offices.

She wasn't home much. Home was basically where she slept between shifts.

Good thing Grandpa Johnny (Mom's dad) lived with us.

He was a wacky old guy. He used to be a rodeo clown and a test pilot for the U.S. Air Force. That was before he invented Velcro, but his partner totally ripped him off, so he never made a penny off it. After that disaster, Grandpa Johnny found his true calling and opened a string of bakeries called Johnny's Cakes, which made him a million dollars, all of which he lost "when the bottom fell out of the cupcake market," he said. "It made a mess—all those cupcakes with no bottoms, just frosting."

At least that's what Grandpa Johnny told Michael and me, because he knew it would crack us up.

Mom told us "the truth." That her father used to own a diner downtown called Johnny's.

"It had the most amazing pastries and cakes," she told me.

Mom had waitressed at her dad's diner when she was in high school. Unfortunately, Grandpa's landlord jacked up his rent, and Johnny's went out of business.

But every day after school, Grandpa Johnny would bake chocolate chip cookies for Michael and me. When it was cold out, we'd get hot cocoa with them. In the spring and summer, he'd make us a chocolate egg cream, which is a fizzy drink with no eggs or cream, just chocolate sauce, milk, and seltzer water.

I remember one afternoon, out of the blue, Grandpa told Michael, "You're such a funny kid. You have a way with words. You make me laugh."

"Um, thanks, I guess," said Michael, because he wasn't used to getting compliments.

Then Grandpa turned to me. "David, you and Michael are going to be friends for life. I guarantee it. Remember where you heard it first."

Grandpa, of course, was totally right.

10

Very Weird Science

Hanging out after school with Grandpa Johnny on a semiregular basis got us both thinking the same thing: maybe we weren't the total losers everybody said we were.

"You know what," I said to Michael, "we should do something that shows the whole school, once and for all, that we're not just a pair of numbskulls."

I said this after Michael and I had both scarfed down like a half a dozen of Grandpa's chocolate chip cookies. We'd also guzzled two cups of hot cocoa. So maybe it was the chocolate talking, but we were pumped.

"We need to show them that we're not really Pottymouth and Stoopid."

"Yeah," muttered Michael, "because that frizzlegristle school is nothing but a bunch of hoopiedoodle flufferknuckles."

"True. So true. But how do we prove that we're not lamebrains?"

"I dunno," mumbled Michael.

"Yeah. Me neither."

We thought for a few minutes.

"Could we be good at sports instead?" Michael asked.

"We tried that," I reminded him. "It didn't go so well."

"How about class presidents?"

"People have to vote for you," I said.

"Sludgepuggle."

"Totally."

We kept thinking. We even tried Googling, but we didn't find any good ideas. Google may have all the answers, but it doesn't know what it's really like to be a kid.

Finally, after more thinking, we both had the same brainstorm at the same time.

We need ANNA BRITANNICA!

"Anna's super-smart," I said.

"She'll know what to do," Michael said.

So we biked over to her house, which was just around the corner from my house.

We were right. Anna knew exactly what we should do.

"The science fair," she said. "It's in two weeks. We could work together and do something amazingly cool."

"I could dunk a basketball off my skateboard," I said.

"Uh, it should probably be something a little more scientific," said Anna.

"With molecules and junk?" asked Michael.

Anna nodded. "Yeah. Molecules."

"Sludgepuggle."

Anna snapped her fingers. "We could make a tornado in a bottle!"

"Really?" I said. "What if it got out?"

"It's not a real tornado, David. But it does demonstrate the vortex principle. It'll be absolutely fabulous. With swirling glitter and smoke..."

"Cool," I said. "Like a fireworks show."

"In a bottle," added Michael. "Awesome."

Anna told us what supplies we needed; all of them were pretty simple to find. She already had the glitter because she liked doing paintings of unicorns and apparently you need a lot of glitter for those.

Michael and I just had to dig up a good juice bottle, some safety matches, dishwasher liquid, and an air pump (like the one we used to inflate our basketball).

This was going to be so amazing. In two weeks, the whole school would finally see us for who we were.

No more Pottymouth, Stoopid, and Anna Britannica.

After the science fair, we would be the three Tornado Masters!

11

The Blame Game

When you're Pottymouth and Stoopid, you get blamed for all sorts of stuff you didn't actually do.

Remember that disgusting lunch in the cafeteria?

The mystery meat in the mushy sauce on a bed of rice that might've been moving? The one everybody called "When You Find Out What It Is, Don't Tell Me"?

Well, somehow, that was our fault.

"Stoopid gave them

the recipe," went the rumor. "And Pottymouth told them to pour schnizzleflick all over it."

When the basketball team lost its first game, everybody blamed Michael.

"Pottymouth called the other team flufferknuckles. That's why we lost. He fired up the enemy with his pottymouthing!"

Not true, of course, but the truth seldom has anything to do with a good Pottymouth or Stoopid story.

For instance, did you know that I'm the one who opened the hamster cage in the fifth-grade classroom and set Scruffy free? Yeah, I didn't know it either. From what I heard, I saw the word *ham* on the cage. I thought there was a sandwich inside and I was hungry.

Run, little furry sandwich, run!

Then there was that disastrous field trip to the natural history museum. The trip when the whole *Tyrannosaurus rex* skeleton in the lobby toppled to the ground. They say I yanked out an anklebone so I could take it home to my dog.

I don't even have a dog, I told anybody who'd listen. Which would be nobody.

When Anna started hanging out with us, she got blamed for stuff too.

The power outage during the big vampire battle scene in the movie everybody was watching during study hall?

"Anna Britannica pulled the plug on the extension cord," proclaimed Kaya Kennecky. "She thought it was a bright orange Twizzler and tried to eat it."

And so it went. Day after day.

Pottymouth did this. Stoopid did that. Anna Britannica did everything else.

I realized that Michael and I had been Pottymouth and Stoopid for so long, most of the kids at school didn't know our real names.

That was okay, I guess.

Because we didn't want to know their names either.

12

All Shapes and Sizes

When you think about bullies in middle school, you probably picture a gnarly mouth-breather with a huge head and a tree-stump neck.

Well, at our school, we have a pair of extremely vicious bullies: Kaya Kennecky (yep, she hasn't changed a bit since pre-K) and Tiffany Blurke.

BULLYUS TYPICALLUS

That's right. They're both girls, not muscle-bound boys.

Day in and day out, those two girls picked on Anna Brittoni without mercy. Most of the junk they pulled took place during gym class. They hid her school clothes so she had to go to class in stinky workout gear. They poured baby oil on the floor in front of her locker. They filled her back-pack with shaving cream. They stole her Snickers bar and refilled the wrapper with wet newspaper.

Then one day in the cafeteria, Kaya and Tiffany went too far.

When Anna wasn't looking, they snatched her most prized possession—her basketball scorebook—and sent it down the dirty-tray line. It was like running a paperback book through a car wash without a car. The thing was soaked, trashed, mangled, and mashed.

Anna had spent hours recording every single shot of every single game in that book. Now the pages were all glued together and covered with smushed lima beans.

Of course, Kaya and Tiffany denied everything.

"She did it herself," they whined to Mrs. Rattner, who was on cafeteria duty that day. "She left it on her tray accidentally on purpose just so she could blame us."

Anna was furious but she didn't show it. She just went back to class and kept scoring 100s and getting A-pluses on everything the school threw at her.

But Michael and I knew Anna was really hurt.

We also knew that she'd just learned what

we'd learned a long time ago: Fly under the radar. Keep a low profile. That way, you make yourself a smaller target.

"If you stay invisible," said Michael, "it's harder for the snifflefliggly flufferknuckles to take shots at you."

Anna had a saying of her own: "Revenge is a dish best served cold."

At first, I thought she was talking about the corn dogs in the cafeteria because they're like fake-meat Popsicles wrapped in pre-chewed Fritos.

But a few days after the "incident" with Anna's scorebook, there was another "incident." One that everybody talked about for weeks.

Because it happened to two of the school's prettiest, most popular people.

Kaya and Tiffany.

13

How to Get Even

At first, Michael and I wondered why Anna would come to school with a roll of plastic wrap.

Was it for some kind of science experiment about osmosis or nonporous surfaces?

Was she wrapping sandwiches in one of her classes? If so, how lame was *that* class?

"Maybe she's just gone hyper-clean," said Michael. "She wants to wrap all her pens, pencils, and junk in plastic to keep 'em sterile. Maybe, with enough plastic wrap, she can seal out the grizzlegoop germs that cause bad breath too."

Then we heard about the "unfortunate incident" in the girls' locker room.

It seems somebody stretched a sheet of clear plastic across both of the toilet seats right before Kaya and Tiffany went into the stalls. Of course Kaya and Tiffany were always the first ones to use the two toilets right after gym class. None of the other girls were allowed to relieve themselves until after the big two did number one.

Funny thing about plastic wrap. If you stretch it tight enough across a toilet, it sort of becomes invisible. Especially when the toilet seat is down, and when it comes to bathrooms, girls always want the toilet seat down (or so my mom tells me on a regular basis).

Anyway, there was, shall we say, a problem. Kaya and Tiffany both ended up with gym shorts that became used diapers. Within an hour, their accident in the girls' locker room turned into the "unfortunate incident."

Anna confessed to the crime.

"Call it revenge," she told the vice principal.

"Therefore, it was served cold."

She was sent home immediately—but not before she donated the rest of her plastic wrap to the cafeteria. "Use it for the leftover corn dogs," she told them. "It'll stop them from tasting like whatever you keep in your freezer that you probably shouldn't."

Principal Ferguson and Vice Principal Driscoll gave Anna only a half-day suspension. She was instructed to report back to school the very next morning because that's when we'd be taking some more state tests. If Anna didn't take them, the average score at our school would probably drop by three points.

Yeah, Anna Britannica is *that* smart.

Anyway, after that we were treated to an afternoon filled with serious discussions.

"We need to talk about this, kids," said Ms. Funkleberger, our social studies teacher, who everybody said was a real-life hippie. "What Anna did was sooooo wrong."

Ms. Funkleberger was probably sixty-something years old with frizzy hair and granny glasses tinted pink. Most of her clothes were tie-dyed.

"So let's rap," she said to the class. "Let it all hang out."

"Why did Anna have to be so mean to poor Kaya and Tiffany?" this one girl asked. "What'd they ever do to her?"

Plenty, I wanted to say. But I didn't. Because I fly under the radar, remember?

"I don't get it," said a guy. "It's crazy. *She's* crazy."

"That Anna girl is weird," said another girl, a friend of Kaya's. "She writes a million numbers in a notebook during every single basketball game. I'm sorry, but that is a sign of a true wackadoodle weirdo."

Yeah, most of the other kids in Ms. Funkleberger's class couldn't understand why anybody would play such a mean trick on sweet Kaya and Tiffany.

Michael and me?

We totally got it.

14

Science Fair-y Tale

Let's jump ahead to the science fair.

You should know we scrapped the tornado-in-a-bottle dealio. We started playing with it, but the "tornado" just looked like a lot of stuff being swirled together, like we were making chocolate milk with glitter and water instead of, you know, chocolate and milk.

We decided to do something that would make us middle-school heroes: we would totally fix the school cafeteria.

The main problem was that the line to get food

moved too slow. Our solution? Zip Trays!

We yanked a few wheels off my old skateboards and bolted them to the bottom of a cafeteria tray. Okay, we probably should've told the cafeteria ladies we were borrowing a tray, but we were sure that when they saw our invention, they would be so happy they wouldn't give us any grief.

Since the science fair was being held in the cafetorium (which is this weird made-up name they have for the big room where we eat lunch because there's a stage on one side and a chow line on the other), it'd be easy to show off our new invention.

But speedy Zip Trays weren't our only improvement. Everyone in the school agreed that the corn dogs in the cafeteria tasted like those frozen wieners wrapped in cold pancakes they sell at the supermarket. So Michael came up with the idea to serve low-cost and delicious *gourmet* corn dogs.

Michael's foster parents are too lazy to cook, so he fixes most of the food at his house. He's really good at it too. His corn dogs are made with chili and cheese. And *bacon.*

On the day of the science fair, we decided to dress up. Anna and I wore our best outfits. Michael wore a toque (that's what French people call the tall white chef hat).

We set up a card table right where the food counter starts. Anna stood next to our trifold board labeled *The Middle-School Cafeteria of the Future*. I was stationed at the tray rails to demonstrate the Zip Tray. Michael was down the line, behind the counter, ready to serve up samples of gourmet corn dogs.

Unfortunately, all the other science fair exhibits were set up on tables all the way on the other side of the cafetorium. Nobody came over to visit our booth.

But that all changed when Michael took the lid off his first tray of corn dogs!

One whiff of that bacon-y, cheesy chili deliciousness and exhibitors abandoned their projects to form a line at Anna's card table.

"Welcome to the cafeteria of the future," she said to like three dozen kids who were frantically sniffing the air like Rottweilers in a Snausages factory.

"What's that smell?" asked one.

"New and improved chili-cheese corn dogs with bacon," said Anna, tapping Michael's recipe, which was displayed on one of our boards. "And now you don't have to wait for speedy service." She gestured toward me. "Introducing the Zip Tray!"

I took a step forward.

"Allow me to demonstrate," I said, just like we'd rehearsed.

But nobody was in the mood for a demonstration. Bacon drives kids crazy.

They wanted Michael's corn dogs...*now!*

When a Good Idea
Goes Bad

"**G**et out of the way, Stoopid," said Jason Cameron, this big guy who'd been calling me Stoopid ever since second grade.

He'd been huge back then too. Everybody said he had a gland problem.

"But this is our main invention," I explained, showing the wheels on the tray. "In the cafeteria of the future, you use this Zip Tray to quickly slide your tray down the line to the delicious corn dogs."

"Well this ain't the future, Stoopid!"

And then Jason picked me up, sat me down on the tray, and gave me a good shove sideways.

The good news was that my invention worked really well. I sped down the food line in like two seconds flat. The bad news was that there was nothing to stop the tray at the end of the counter. I flew off the tray rails and smashed onto the very hard, very sticky cafeteria floor.

That wasn't part of the plan.

"Give me a corn dog, Pottymouth!" snarled Jason. "With extra bacon and double cheese."

"You were supposed to use the Zip Tray, you flufferknuckle," Michael said. "That's half of the whole hicklesnicklepox science project."

"What'd you call me?"

"A flufferknuckle!"

Jason frowned. "What's that?"

"What *you* are."

I was glad to see that Michael didn't back down.

But now, the crowd was five-deep for dogs. "Just give us our food, Pottymouth!" they were shouting.

Michael stood behind the counter, unsure what to do next.

This was when Kaya Kennecky stepped forward and, since she was a cheerleader, started leading a cheer.

"Give me a *C*, give me an *O*, give me an *R-N D-O-G!* What's that spell?"

It took most of the kids like five seconds to

figure that one out. "Um, *corn dog!*" the mob finally shouted. "Give me a corn dog!"

Hands reached over the sneezeguards. Elbows flew. Some guys climbed on top of the tray rails and leaped over the glass partition so they could raid Michael's tray.

"Get your hoopiedoodle paws off my sniffle-piggle corn dogs, you hornswogglers!"

The mob kept chanting and grabbing corn dogs and shoving one another.

Michael had no choice but to retreat. The corn-dog tray clattered to the floor. Somebody knocked over our cardboard display. Somebody else started using my Zip Tray to skateboard around the kitchen equipment.

And, of course, that's exactly when the judges came in to grade our exhibit.

Everybody just froze and acted innocent.

"And what have we here?" asked Vice Principal Driscoll.

"Something totally stupid for a science fair," cracked Kaya. "Corn dogs aren't exactly scientific."

"B-b-but…" sputtered Anna.

Kaya propped her fists on her hips and pouted at one of the teachers, Mr. Stafford.

"Mr. Stafford, you're a science teacher. Are corn dogs even an invention?"

"Well, I suppose they were, at one point, before the first cook skewered the first hot dog on a stick and dipped it into a vat of cornbread batter, but I fail to see…"

Long story short?

Our science project was a complete bust. I lost my Zip Tray (the skateboarding kid never came back). We were written up for unauthorized use of school property. Nobody read Anna's display board about the cafeteria of the future even though there was all sorts of good stuff on it about healthier food choices and improving the speed of service.

We didn't win any ribbons. Everybody hated us even though they ate all of our corn dogs. Plus, we had to buy the school a new tray to replace the one that dude skated away on.

Once again, the whole school was laughing at

us. But we were used to that. Hey, it's what we do.

We're Pottymouth, Stoopid, and Anna Britan-nica.

We get laughed at.

16

Living Up to Our Names

After the science fair fiasco, Michael and I got really, really mad at the whole world.

And you know what? In our humble opinions, the whole world totally deserved it. (And since you were probably in the world back then, I guess that means we were mad at you too. Sorry about that. Our bad.)

We were both so angry we started "acting out," as the school psychologists call it. We called it something else: payback time.

We went to work.

Michael has always been pretty good at imitating voices. He does a mean Homer, not to mention an awesome Family Guy. One day, I went to see the school secretary, Mrs. Tuttafacio.

"The vending machine ate all my coins and left my Goobers dangling," I told her. Mrs. Tuttafacio sighed heavily and then went with me to the cafeteria, muttering, "How stupid can one boy be?" the whole way.

The second the coast was clear, Michael went in, grabbed the PA microphone (which looks a lot like a telephone), and made a few announcements—sounding exactly like Principal Ferguson!

Everyone was super-confused. It was great.

Another time, I was so mad, I went absolutely nutso when my locker wouldn't unlock even after I'd done the combination fifteen times in a row.

Like I said, we were mad.

The corner convenience store had *Mad* magazine on its magazine rack.

"Get out of my figgledybiggledy face, Alfred E. Neuman!" said Michael.

Yeah. We were even mad at *Mad*.

"I think we're going to end up in reform school," I told Michael right after we got so mad at a pile of dog poop sitting in the middle of the sidewalk that we kicked it out of our way. (Okay, that *was* stupid.)

"Reform school or worse," said Michael. "Much worse."

Our Future's So Bright, We Gotta Wear Chains

We both kept getting madder and madder, angrier and angrier.

You try being called Pottymouth and Stoopid by everybody from the age of four on. It'll make you bitter. So will sucking a dozen lemons dry in a day, but Michael and I did that only once because nobody on our block had a spare buck to buy it. We had to do something with all those lemons. At least we had a pound of sugar too.

This one time, we were walking home after school with Anna, and we started imagining

what the rest of our lives would look like.

Think old prison movie. In black-and-white. Then add in a very spooky dun-dun-*duuuuun* sound track.

Our future didn't seem very bright. In fact, it looked pretty grim. The color of dirty dishwater, something Michael and I figured we'd better get used to since we seemed destined for careers as dishwashers. Or busboys. By the way, can girls grow up to be busboys? Because Anna needed a job too.

"Fudging school cafeteria is where we'll end up," said Michael.

"You could be a chef like David's grandpa Johnny!" said Anna, who still clung to a shred of hope because she hadn't been Anna Britannica as long as Michael and I had been Pottymouth and Stoopid. "You could open a gourmet corn-dog stand!"

"No bifflebusting way," said Michael. "I'll be wearing a baseball cap asking flufferknuckles if they want fries with that for the rest of my life."

"And what if they want onion rings with that?" I said. "Why doesn't anybody ever ask if I want onion rings? Or Tater Tots?"

"I think I'll grow up to be a super-smart

homeless person," said Anna. "I could give people little-known facts for spare change."

The 3 Musketeers bar was originally split into three pieces each with different flavors: vanilla, chocolate, and strawberry.

Alaska is the only state that can be typed on one row of keys.

Obsessive nose picking is called rhinotillexomania.

Will Provide Useless Information for Food.

"If you're homeless," I said, "Michael and I could be homeless with you. We could start our own cardboard condo complex."

"That'd be so cool," said Michael. "We could all have boxes next to each other."

"I'd like a refrigerator crate," I said. "Those things are sturdy."

"I want one of those wardrobe boxes," said

Anna. "The kind moving companies have. With the rod to hang stuff up."

"I want one of those too," I said. "I could use the rod to dry out my socks on rainy days. Of course, if it's raining, I guess our cardboard walls would bend."

"Doesn't matter," said Michael. "A box like that with a rod would be awesometastic. Like living in a closet, but without any stinkerrific mothballs. My foster mom mothballs everything. It's why I smell like an old person's attic."

Now all three of us were cracking up.

"And after we're homeless for a while," I said, "we'll probably go to jail."

"The dunkiedooking Big House," said Michael.

Anna looked thoughtful. "But behind bars, we'll learn a trade."

"License-plate printing?" he asked.

"We'll learn our state's dumb nickname. Over and over and over."

"Hicklesnicklepox depressing," said Michael.

I nodded. "We have so much to look forward to."

If You Can't Beat 'Em, Join 'Em...and Get Beat

Pretty soon, we were so mad, we decided to take it out on other kids.

That's right. We became bullies.

Well, we *tried* to.

We figured everybody at school was afraid of the bullies (us included), so maybe if we were bullies, all the other kids would be so terrified of what we might do to them that they'd stop calling us Pottymouth and Stoopid.

But it didn't work out that way.

Michael and me? Worst. Bullies. Ever.

We didn't know what we were supposed to do or how to do it. We couldn't tell a swirly-whirly from an atomic wedgie, a triple-nipple cripple from a raspberry rug burn.

We even studied those signs they have all over school, the ones that explain what bullying is.

We hung out on the playground and looked for kids who seemed like they wouldn't put up much of a fight. Small kids. Kids with glasses or those spiky dinosaur backpacks. Then we'd go over and ignore them in a mean way.

"Why are you ignoring me like that?" said our first victim, a tiny kid named Sherman. He didn't look like he weighed much more than a cat.

"It's what we bullies do," I said.

"This whole school is a no-bullying zone, buster," said Sherman. "Consider this fair warning."

"Um, fair warning about what?" I asked.

"I won't tolerate bullying," said Sherman. "If I see something, I'm going to say something. I might even *do* something!"

Michael got a pained look on his face. I think he had gas. Sherman thought it was a snarl. It sort of made the little guy snap.

He screamed "Hi-*ya!*" and leaped into a pretty awesome martial-arts stance.

Turned out Sherman goes to karate class every day after school. Weekends too.

It also turned out that Michael and I ended up on our butts.

Like I said: Worst. Bullies. Ever.

Nicknames Run
in the Family

"This bullying thing?" said Grandpa Johnny one day after school, "not the smartest thing you've ever done, David."

"So," I sort of growled, because we were still mad at the whole world, and Grandpa Johnny was *in* the world, "are you going to start calling me Stoopid too?"

"Nah," he said. "That's not the right nickname for you. You're far too smart to be a Stoopid. You're more of a Dave-o. Or Speedball. Maybe Scooter."

"Scooter?"

Grandpa Johnny shrugged. "I like watching you two boys play basketball on your skateboard. It reminds me of this scooter I used to fly around town on when I was your age. I always wanted to be called Scooter!"

"Well, what about me?" said Michael, talking with his mouth full of food, which is against the rules with most adults but not Grandpa Johnny. "Am I supposed to be Pottymouth for the rest of my life?"

"Nope," said Grandpa Johnny. "Right now, I'd call you Cookiemouth. Or Crumbcrusher. But if you two keep trying to bully kids who are smaller and weaker than you, I'll end up just calling you Crummy because it's a lousy thing to do, Michael."

For whatever reason, the way Grandpa Johnny said that while frowning and wagging his bony finger at us made us all crack up. He was the one guy in the whole world who totally got me and Michael. He was someone we could both talk to. And he always baked us cookies, which made the talking a whole lot easier.

"You know, over the years, I've had a few nicknames myself," said Grandpa Johnny, leaning back in his chair and remembering.

"Like what?" we asked.

"Let's see. In grade school, I was Boogers."

"How'd you get that nickname?"

"Take a wild guess. When I was in school, I was called the Groove."

"What does that mean?" I asked.

Grandpa laughed. "It means I had some fine moves on the dance floor, especially if the band played soul music. In the navy, where I first learned to cook, they called me Sea Biscuits and Gravy."

Michael and I had to smile. Who knew nicknames could be fun instead of just plain evil?

"Your grandmother?" he said to me, his eyes moistening slightly because Grandma Joanne passed before I was even born. "I used to call her Cookie."

"Did she do all the cooking at home?" asked Michael.

"Are you kidding? The woman couldn't boil water. But she was one smart cookie. I think that's where you get *your* brains, David."

Grandpa Johnny was forever telling me how smart I was. Guess he didn't get the memo about me being Stoopid.

"What did she call you?" asked Michael.

"Stretch," said Grandpa Johnny without missing a beat. "Because I'm so tall."

We all cracked up again.

Grandpa Johnny was maybe (and I'm being generous here) five feet tall. He'd needed one of those claws on a stick to pull stuff off the highest shelves in his restaurant.

He had like six different step stools he took with him wherever he lived. And he absolutely hated ceiling fans.

Stay on high all winter long, you indoor whirlybird. See if I care!

Things Can Always Get Worse

Michael always says, "Well, at least we know things can't get any worse."

But then, of course, they do.

Grandpa Johnny died.

I don't know how close you are to your grand-parents, but since my dad left when I was so young, I sometimes thought of Grandpa Johnny as my father. Crazy, right? But he was the one who was always there for me. With a smile. A little advice. A plate of fresh-baked cookies.

Grandpa died peacefully, in his sleep, thank goodness. He just went to bed one night and didn't wake up the next morning. I guess we should be happy about that. There wasn't any pain or scary race to the hospital in an ambulance. But I never got to tell him good-bye. Or "Thanks for the cookies." Or "I love you." Or "Catch you later, Stretch."

You know what the last thing I said to my grandfather was?

"See you tomorrow, Grandpa."

I wish I could've said something better for the last time I would ever talk to him.

The second he heard the news, Michael rushed over to see if there was anything he could do for me or Mom.

"Not really," I said. "But thanks."

We both realized that our lives were going to be a lot less interesting without Grandpa Johnny.

"He was just about the only grizzlesnot grown-up who treated us like we were ordinary, hicklesnicklepox kids," said Michael.

Mom was totally choked up when Grandpa

passed because she'd just lost her dad. That was something that I had gone through, more or less, at a much earlier age. Not that my ex-dad was dead, although when Michael and I first found out what he did to us, we both sort of wished he had croaked. For a couple seconds, anyway.

More about what Ex-Dad did later. Promise.

One of my favorite memories of Grandpa Johnny?

Him telling Michael and me that we'd be friends forever. I think he was right.

Anyway, you could definitely say that losing Grandpa was the worst thing that ever happened to Michael and me.

Well, up to that point.

21

Letting Grandpa Down

Since Mom was working three jobs to make ends meet and Grandpa's monthly Social Security check wouldn't be coming anymore, we had to go the bargain route for his funeral.

"I'm sorry, you guys," she told us. "He deserves better."

"It's okay," Michael told her. "Grandpa Johnny wouldn't want you wasting a ton of money on a fancy box you're just going to bury in the dinkledorker dirt."

Anna brought over a casserole of mac and cheese. She figured Mom wouldn't feel much like cooking after spending the day making funeral arrangements.

(Not that Mom was ever home long enough between jobs to actually cook dinner. We're more of a nuke-it-yourself family.)

"You know the guy who invented Pringles?" asked Anna. "He was cremated. They buried his ashes in a Pringles can. True story."

We had the funeral on a Saturday. Not too many people came. Just a few of the folks who used to work for Grandpa at Johnny's Diner. A couple neighbors. The mailman and a lady who, the funeral director told us later, goes to every funeral she can. She even signed the guest book.

We drove from the funeral home to the cemetery in Mom's clunker car. We didn't pay for the package where the grieving family gets to ride in a limo. As we were driving to the cemetery, Mom's classic rock station was invaded by an annoying commercial for Big Bob's Auto Barn.

Hi, folks, this is me, Big Bob from Big Bob's Auto Barn. And no body beats my prices because I'm a-head of the competition. That's right, I said no body. *Because I'm just a head. Floating over all these great deals like a hot-air balloon with hair and a cowboy hat. But you can't see that because this is a radio commercial.*

Yeah. It was the one my ex-dad wrote. It was also totally lame.

At the gravesite, a preacher droned on about how we're all made out of dust and "to dust we shall return."

Made me wonder why people clean their rooms or dust stuff. Seems kind of disrespectful.

Then it started to rain, which was fine with me. Fit my mood perfectly.

I also had the distinct feeling that the preacher didn't really know Grandpa.

For one thing, he called him Jimmy until Mom whispered, "It's Johnny."

Of course, Grandpa never really went to church all that much. Just Christmas and Easter. Sometimes. It depended on when the service started. And whether it was snowing. Or raining. Or if he'd stayed up too late the night before watching holiday specials on cable TV.

There was one special guest star for the funeral. And, of course, he showed up late.

My ex-dad.

I told you we'd get back to him.

A Funny Thing Happened After Grandpa's Funeral

When the preacher checked his watch and said, "That concludes our service," Ex-Dad shuffled over to Mom.

He held his arms open like he wanted to comfort her with a big ol' bear hug.

Mom (looking like she might hurl) took two quick steps back. One more and she would've tripped over Grandpa's coffin and ended up six feet under.

Mom wasn't interested in hugging any bears, especially not my ex-dad. I couldn't blame her.

Bears usually stink like whatever they just rolled around in.

"What are you doing here, Tony?" Mom asked.

"I wanted to be here. For you. And your dad."

"Why?"

"Because I liked the old guy."

"Really? He wasn't too crazy about you."

"Sure he was."

"No, Tony. He wasn't. Trust me on this one. He used to call you Tony Baloney."

Michael, Anna, and I sniggered a little when Mom said that. We liked it when she got feisty.

"We should talk," said Ex-Dad.

"We really should," said Mom. "First subject, child-support payments."

"How's David doing?" Ex-Dad asked, as if I weren't standing like four feet behind him. I could tell; he was definitely trying to change the subject to anything besides the money he owed my mom.

"To be honest," said Mom, "David's not so great. He and his best friend, Michael, are having a hard time at school. They have these horrible nicknames. It's made things pretty miserable for them both."

"Really?" said Ex-Dad. "What kind of nick-names?"

"I don't like repeating them."

"Come on. Tell me."

Mom sighed. "Michael is Pottymouth. David is Stoopid."

"Pottymouth and Stoopid?"

I couldn't see Ex-Dad's face, but I could hear the smirk in his voice.

"Is David, like, super-dumb or something?" he asked Mom right in front of me. "Do we need to send him to a specialist?"

"No, Tony. In fact, he's extremely bright.

That's why he gets bored so easily and starts doing stuff that causes problems."

"What kind of stuff?"

"I'd rather not talk about it. Especially not here."

"Of course not," said Ex-Dad. And then he kept talking about it. "Does his pottymouth friend swear a lot?"

"No. He just makes up words."

"Like what?" Ex-Dad pressed.

"Hicklesnicklepox and flufferknuckles." She smiled over Ex-Dad's shoulder at Michael.

"Really? What do they mean?"

Mom shrugged. "Nobody knows. Except Michael. And maybe David."

"And the other kids make fun of them because they're so...different? That's hysterical!"

"No, Tony, it's cruel and it's sad."

"It sounds kind of funny to me. Who's the girl?" Ex-Dad nodded toward Anna.

"Anna Brittoni. She's their friend. The kids at school call her Anna Britannica."

Ex-Dad snickered. "They have a lot of cute nicknames at this school, huh?"

"No, Tony. There's nothing cute about this. It's ugly."

Ex-Dad turned to me. "Hey, David—what'd you do to become Stoopid?"

I shrugged. "Just some dumb stuff, I guess."

"Like what?"

"I dunno."

"Come on. I'm your father." Technically, he was right, but he definitely wasn't a *dad*.

"Tell me, son," he said.

Yeah. He went there. He played the "son" card. And I fell for it.

"Well," I said, toeing the grass, "one time, in kindergarten, I put a stick in the pencil sharpener because I thought it would be easier to toast marshmallows if the stick was pointier."

Dad started laughing.

"It wasn't all that funny, sir," said Michael.

"No," said Ex-Dad. "But come on—it *was* pretty stupid."

Michael balled up his fists. His face turned purple. He couldn't hold it in.

"David is not stupid, you snifflepiggle, frizzle-gristle flufferknuckle!"

Ex-Dad cracked up. "That was hysterical, Pottymouth! Hysterical!"

He couldn't stop laughing. He was doubled over, holding his sides.

In a *graveyard*. Right after my grandpa's funeral.

I could tell Mom was as steamed as I was. She stomped toward her car as quickly as she could. "Come on, kids. Let's go home."

We hurried after her.

"You know, David," Mom said through tightly clenched teeth, "I'm starting to remember why I couldn't stand being around your ex-father."

"Yeah," I added. "Me too."

Behind us, though, I could still hear Ex-Dad laughing his head off. "This is hilarious!" he cried to no one. "I'm sorry, but, come on, it's priceless. *Pottymouth and Stoopid!*"

Yeah. That's the guy who was supposed to be my dad.

23

Sharing Is Caring

About a week later, Ex-Dad sent Mom some of the money he owed her for child support. Not all of it. Some. Still, I guess it was a start.

"And," he told her on the phone, "I want to take David and his friend Michael out to lunch this weekend. Someplace special."

"You do?" Mom was sort of shocked. Money in the mail and a free meal for the kids? How lucky could she get? I'm guessing she went out and played her lottery numbers that day.

"I shouldn't've laughed at those awful nicknames those terrible kids at school call David and Michael. That was totally insensitive of me. I want to make it up to them."

So Mom went ahead and said yes, and, on a sunny Saturday, Ex-Dad drove over to pick me and Michael up (in a car wrapped in a gigantic Big Bob's Auto Barn ad).

Our *special* lunch spot?

McDonald's.

"You guys grab a booth," he told us. "I'll grab us some grub."

He went to the counter to place the order. Michael and I found a table near the window.

"This is pretty dinkatastic decent of him," said Michael.

"I guess," I replied. "But he didn't ask either of us what we wanted to eat."

Michael shrugged. "It's all good."

Ex-Dad came to our booth with a tray. "I got you guys fries," he said proudly. "*Large* fries."

He set the tray on the table, and, yeah, that's exactly what he'd gotten us: one large order of fries, plus three dozen ketchup and salt packets.

"Help yourself to all the condiments you want, kids. They're free. So tell me more about this Pottymouth and Stoopid business. What's up with that?"

"What other kinds of dumb stuff have you done, son?" asked Ex-Dad, helping himself to one of our fries.

"I'd rather not talk about it."

"Come on. Dads need to know what happens to their sons."

"Well, there was the time Michael and I decided to have a snowball fight. In April. We used mud."

Ex-Dad laughed. "That's so stupid, it's brilliant! Do you play any, you know, stupid sports?"

"Just Skateboardball, I guess. Some kids think it's stupid."

"We don't," added Michael

"Well, what is it?" asked Ex-Dad.

"This game we made up," I told him. "It's like basketball but with skateboards."

Ex-Dad kept pumping us for more stories. When the fries were all gone, he splurged and bought us a refill. He also got us a McFlurry. *One.* With two spoons.

"So tell me about the science fair," said Ex-Dad. "I hear you wrapped a corn dog in bacon or something."

Since we were sort of stuck there, we told him all about the science fair disaster with the Zip Tray and the chili-cheese-bacon corn dogs. Then

Michael rattled off a list of all the words he'd made up. After that, Ex-Dad told us a few stories about the jerks he had to work with at his advertising agency. It was pretty funny stuff.

"But don't worry, boys," he said with a wink. "One day, I'm going to shake the dust of that crummy little ad agency off my shoes and leave those hacks behind. You'll see. I'm gonna hit it big, kids. I've got a few projects I'm shopping around right now. Just waiting for the right one to land on the right desk. I'll be a bazillionaire."

"Awesome," I said. "Then maybe you could send Mom the rest of the money you owe her so she doesn't have to work three jobs?"

"Sounds like a plan."

Since all of a sudden he was acting like a semi-decent human being who cared about me and Mom, Michael and I told him more stories. Before long, we were all laughing like crazy.

"A couple times," said Michael, "I snagged the PA system and imitated Principal Ferguson's voice. Once, I told everybody to go home early because zombie Martians had invaded! The whole

school was halfway out the door before Principal Ferguson came running out of the staff bathroom with toilet paper stuck to his shoe to let everybody know the Martians weren't really invading and didn't want to suck everybody's brains out of their ears with straws!"

"Hysterical," said Ex-Dad. "You guys are amazing!"

I went ahead and told him some of the extremely stupid stunts I'd pulled over the years. "One time, I licked the flagpole in front of my elementary school to see if my tongue would get stuck. It didn't. It was the middle of summer."

We told Ex-Dad so many stories, he had to get us a McFlurry refill too.

Finally, maybe three hours after we ate our first french fry, Ex-Dad took us back to Mom's house.

"We should do this more often," he said.

As he pulled away, we could tell that he was laughing his head off again.

"Your ex-dad is actually kind of cool," said Michael.

"Yeah," I said. "Like an ice storm in Antarctica."

But a little part of me couldn't help hoping that maybe, just maybe, he'd start being a real dad and not an ex-.

TONY SCUNGILI

David's "Ex-Dad"

Right after I saw David and Michael at the funeral, it hit me. This was a big idea.

A *huge* idea.

The biggest idea I've ever had in my life, even though it wasn't actually my idea.

Actually, it doesn't matter where the idea came from. Does anybody care where Hemingway got the idea for *The Old Man and the Sea*? Probably from an old man he knew. Or maybe the sea.

The point is—this idea was G-I-G-A-N-T-I-C!

It was also going to make me a millionaire.

All my life, I've been a frustrated novelist, a frustrated screenwriter, and a frustrated human being. Well, I was ready to say good-bye to writing cheesy ads for Big Bob's Auto Barn.

So I took David and his friend—Martin? Matthew? Whatever—out for a nice lunch and grabbed a few more stories to use. They were walking, talking gold mines of funny stuff.

I pitched my big idea to the guys at the Cartoon Factory in Chicago. They looooved it, just like I knew they would. *They* said it was going to be *ginormous!*

They also said they would pay me a *huge* sum of money.

I liked when they said that.

24

Michael Nearly Gets a Sort-Of Girlfriend. Almost

I should mention that life wasn't totally bleak for Michael and me. Every now and then, the clouds of doom over our heads would part and we'd actually see a ray of sunshine.

For instance, one day, Michael met this girl at the 7-Eleven. She was ahead of him in line at the checkout counter but she couldn't make up her mind about what kind of gum she wanted.

"I can't really chew it," she muttered, her hand hovering over the display case. "Not for six more months. I'm just buying it and saving it."

"Whatever," said the ever-helpful slacker dude behind the counter, who was busy fiddling with his phone.

"What flavor is the one with the blue and pink wrapper?" asked the girl.

"Gum," said the guy.

"What about that green one?"

"Gum."

Michael decided to jump in and help. "The blue and pink one tastes like birthday cake. And that green one's wasabi-flavored. Completely scorched my postnasal drippage."

The girl looked over at him. "This one says it tastes like papaya-mango-boysenberry-mint. Is that a good thing?"

"Totally," said Michael. "Boysenberry sounds kind of weird but nice, huh?"

She grinned and said, "You're kind of weird and nice too." (Okay, that's what Michael *told* me she said.)

When she smiled, Michael noticed something: her mouth was full of braces.

The girl's name, Michael discovered, was

Emma, even though nobody at school called her that. "They call me, let's see..." She started ticking off the names on her fingers. "Metal Mouth, Brace Face, Cheese Grater, Train Tracks, Barbed Wire..."

Michael couldn't believe his ears. Not only was this girl talking to him like he was a normal person, but one of her nicknames (Metal Mouth) was pretty close to his.

"I wish I could still chew gum," she said.

"I have an idea," said Michael. "Why don't I buy the gum and chew it for you? I can tell you what it tastes like."

"Really? You'd describe it?"

"Yeah. They say I, uh, have a way with words."

So every day after school for, like, a week, Michael and Emma would try out a new pack of gum. Michael would chew it and then use his made-up words to describe it.

"This one is puckerfully fruitatious," Michael would tell her. "This one is zingtastically face-blastastic."

Michael was really happy. He had a new friend who just happened to be a super-nice (and cute) girl. They even hung out together at school.

Then Emma found out that Michael was actually Pottymouth.

"That's you?" Emma gasped. "*Eww!* I can't believe I let you contaminate my ears." She crinkled her nose like she could smell his foul language. "Everybody says you're disgusting and evil."

"Well," said Michael, "those are the same pooperrific people who call you Metal Mouth."

"So? My braces are coming off in six months. There's no way to fix what's wrong with *your* mouth. My life's not nearly as suckerrific as yours. Thanks for helping me see that."

"You're not welcome. Have a really nice, fun hicklesnicklepox life, Emma."

And once again, the clouds closed over our heads and started dumping buckets of rain.

Excuuuuuse Me
for Living

Speaking of girls, I met one too.

Kind of.

I went to the movies by myself. I'd saved up the money for a while, ever since I knew this film was coming out. Michael usually goes with me but this was during his gum-describing days with Emma so I was flying solo. And since it was a Saturday afternoon, Anna was busy studying at the public library. (Nobody made fun of her there.)

Anyway, I was sitting in the darkened theater,

all alone, snug in my seat, waiting for stuff to start blowing up on the screen. I crinkled open the bag of microwaved popcorn I'd snuck into the theater because, come on, who can afford to buy the stuff they sell at the concession stand? At a movie theater, you can buy food-court-quality nachos for the price of a whole meal at a real Mexican restaurant. In Mexico.

I was munching away, enjoying the trailer for a new animated movie about flying pigs made by "the gang of knuckleheads at the Cartoon Factory," this super-popular cable channel all the kids at school love. The stuff they put out is laugh-your-butt-off funny.

Anyway, I was just about settled in when somebody scooted up my row and accidentally stomped on my foot.

"Oops," she said. "Excuse me."

I looked up.

It was an extremely cute girl. Plus, she had to be rich. She had half of the concession stand cradled in her arms.

After she said "excuse me," she added, "my bad."

Then she sort of squinted at me. My heart kind of leaped in my chest. I started wondering: *Is this girl going to become my Gum Girl?*

Would I start hanging out with Miss Toe-Stomper?

Could I describe different flavors of micro-waved popcorn to her?

Would she go with me to the Cartoon Factory's flying-pig movie when it came out?

But then the mystery foot stomper's eyes adjusted to the darkness. She saw who the foot she'd nearly crushed belonged to.

"Oh. It's you, Stoopid. Why did you try to trip me with your stupid foot? I can't believe you'd try something so dumb. Is this your stupid idea of a joke?"

What? It was like we were suddenly in a movie scene, one she was making up, and I didn't have the script.

"Usher?" she cried to the guy working his way up the aisles with a swinging flashlight. "This immature boy tried to trip me with his big stupid feet."

My imaginary romance was even shorter than Michael's. The usher shone his flashlight in my face. "How stupid can you be, kid?" the usher asked.

"You have no idea," said the girl as the usher hauled me out of my seat. He didn't even want to hear my side of the story, aka the *truth*.

Two minutes later, the guy in the red blazer tossed me out a side exit, yelling about no refunds. I ended up in an alleyway. It was raining.

And then a passing garbage truck splashed wet gutter slush up on the sidewalk.

Yeah. Those rain clouds were finding all sorts of new ways to dump on me.

DONATELLA SCUNGILI

David's Mom

    I just want to say something about David and Michael.

    Albert Einstein was one of the smartest men who ever lived. But he nearly flunked out of school, probably because none of his teachers knew what to do with him. The same way they don't know what to do with David and Michael.

    Anyway, Einstein apparently once said, "Everybody is a genius. But if you judge a fish by its ability to climb a tree, it will live its whole life believing that it is stupid."

My son, David?

He's that fish.

26

The History of Failure

You might think that, after our experience with the school science fair, we'd stay away from any and all activities with the word *fair* in the name.

You'd be wrong.

Michael, Anna, and I had this awesome idea for the school's history fair, so we went ahead and did it. Actually, it's called History Fair: Parade of Time, and all the students are supposed to dress up as their favorite historical characters, march into the auditorium, and take turns making speeches about what made them famous.

Anna came up with the idea for our historical figures—two guys that Michael and I had never heard of.

"Exactly!" said Anna. "Our project will focus on history's underdogs, the ones that time has forgotten. The quiet people who actually made history while other, louder people made all the headlines and grabbed all the glory. Let's hold up the people who did brilliant things but ended up shoved off to the side because the spotlight was hogged by somebody with a much bigger mouth."

I think she was sort of talking about us. How we might be smart or talented but nobody would notice because they were too busy making fun of us.

Anyway, we all worked together on our script and costumes.

For the history fair, we were going to go as Henry Woodward and Mathew Evans, two inventors from Canada who nobody (including us) had ever heard of before. Michael and I found some fake fur coats and floppy-eared hats at a thrift store and watched a lot of hockey games to work on our Canadian accents. Part of the costume was also this huge lightbulb we'd found in a dumpster behind the novelty shop at the mall.

So who were Woodward and Evans?

In 1874, these two Canadians filed a patent for an electric lightbulb made out of a glass tube with a chunk of carbon inside that was connected to two tiny wires. That's right. They were the guys who *actually* invented the lightbulb, not Thomas Alva Edison.

There was only one slight problem: Woodward and Evans were totally broke. So they sold their lightbulb patent to Thomas Edison.

The rest, as they say, is history.

Edison put their pieces together, built the first electric lightbulb, and hogged all the credit.

"So, you hosers," I said to the crowded auditorium in my best Canadian accent (I had no idea what a hoser was, but Google said it was a Canadian thing). "The next time you flip on a light switch, be sure you say thank you to Woodward and Evans, eh?"

"And forget that flufferknuckle Edison, eh?" added Michael.

A couple kids in the audience coughed.

One guy shouted, *"Stooooopid!"*

The panel of judges barely paid attention to our presentation. One even went out to use the bathroom while we were onstage. He must've

figured anything created by Pottymouth, Stoopid, and Anna Britannica would be a waste of his time. And guess who came onstage right after us?

A kid dressed up like Thomas Alva Edison. He wore a bow tie and a tweed vest. He'd also put white shoe polish in his hair.

"Hello, everybody," he said, waving a flashlight around. "I'm Thomas Alva Edison! Ignore those losers who were just here. Let there be light, because *I* just invented the lightbulb!"

The applause was deafening.

Michael and I and my floppy-eared hat shuffled off.

"Hicklesnicklepox, eh?" muttered Michael, which made me crack up.

Because he said it in an awesome Canadian accent.

Whhhhhhh-
haaaaaaaat?

Okay, it's time for the big shocker.

I'm coming to the reason we're having this assembly and why people from the Cartoon Factory are following Michael and me around making a documentary about us. Why they're interviewing a bunch of kids and teachers at our school, plus Mom and Ex-Dad.

After the history fair, Michael and Anna came over to hang out.

"We should've won the blue ribbon," said Anna as we passed around a bowl of popcorn.

I just shook my head. "I can't believe they gave it to the Thomas Edison guy. Especially after we told everybody about Woodward and Evans."

Thanks for inventing the alarm clock!

I didn't.

Well, you woke us up after Pottymouth and Stoopid's presentation, so that kind of counts.

Michael shrugged. "Hey, the dude had that flashlight, a record player, *and* a telephone."

"Edison didn't invent the telephone!" said Anna. "That was Alexander Graham Bell!"

Michael shrugged again. "Tell it to the skiffer-deejibberdee judges."

"We definitely had the best presentation," said Anna. "Backed up by the most interesting research."

"So?" I said. "Nobody ever pays attention to the three of us."

"Yes, they do," said Michael. "But only when they're calling us names."

"Or laughing at us," added Anna.

"Right. That too."

I aimed the remote at the TV and clicked the button. It was eight o'clock. The Cartoon Factory network usually had something good on at eight.

That night was no exception.

"Attention, knuckleheads," said the jazzed-up announcer who always sounded like a buck-toothed beaver who'd just downed a double shot of Red Bull. "It's time for a hysterically funny, brand-spankin'-new show. The Cartoon Factory presents the world premiere of *Pottymouth and Stoopid!*"

Jaws dropped.

The popcorn bowl fell to the floor.

We stared at the screen in disbelief as cartoon

letters bounced into each other to spell out our horrible nicknames.

Whhhhhhhhaaaaaaaaat?

28

In Case You Missed It...

L et me repeat that:

Whhhhhhhhaaaaaaaaat?

The *Pottymouth & Stoopid* show started with a wacky theme song that sounded like the *Itchy and Scratchy Show* tune from *The Simpsons*. While some chipmunky voices sang and the title faded away, the two faces in the *Pottymouth & Stoopid* logo morphed into cartoon characters.

Pottymouth and Stoopid? They looked exactly...like Michael and me, only Stoopid's face was orange and Pottymouth's was brown.

The opening credits ended, and there we were: a pair of brown and orange cartoon kids in kindergarten.

A deep-voiced announcer explained: "Pottymouth and Stoopid got their start as A-plus losers way back in preschool, the momentous day they first met."

"Hey, Pottymouth?" said the mini-me.

"Yeah, Stoopid?"

"Want to finger-paint?"

"Let's arm-and-leg-paint instead!"

And we both jumped into paint buckets.

"If you haven't noticed, Pottymouth is famous for making up naughty words," boomed the announcer as the scene shifted to us on an elementary-school playground. "And Stoopid? Well, he's just stupid!"

"Now they're in middle school," said the announcer as the scene shifted again. "And if you didn't think Pottymouth and Stoopid could get any dumber, you are sooooo wrong!"

Pottymouth and Stoopid were hanging out in

a cartoon house's driveway with a basketball hoop over the garage door, just like me and Michael did all the time.

"Hey," said Stoopid. "I have an idea. Let's invent a new sport. Skateboardball!"

And Stoopid raced across the asphalt on his board, took his shot, missed it, and slammed into the garage door. Chirping birds swirled around his head.

"Sludgepuggle," said Pottymouth.

That scene dissolved into another one showing the two cartoon kids flinging mud balls at each other.

"Snowball fights are fun in April," said Stoopid. "Your fingers don't get cold."

"And your nose doesn't dribble grizzlenoogies," said Pottymouth.

After a few more stupid stunts—including the two kids taking turns licking a flagpole—Pottymouth and Stoopid went to school and had some fun tricking the secretary in the front office into deserting her post.

"Hey, Mrs. Toothface," said Stoopid, "the

vending machine in the cafeteria ate my dollar bill."

Mrs. Toothface, who had very big teeth that matched her name, glared at Stoopid over the frames of her funny eyeglasses. "The vending machine in the cafeteria doesn't have a dollar-bill slot."

"I know," said Stoopid. "That's why I stuffed it in the coin slot."

Mrs. Toothface shook her head, grabbed a clinking ring of keys, and stomped out of the office.

"Walk this way, Stoopid."

And then he started waddling the way Mrs. Toothface was waddling. They both looked like hippos in a hurry.

The scene ended with a laugh track yukking it up as Mrs. Toothface got stuck in the doorway. Stoopid had to push her through. The squeaky sound effect for that bit sounded like a balloon going into a box.

"More *Pottymouth and Stoopid*," said the announcer, "right after these words from our sponsors!"

We were in a total state of shock during all the commercials.

Including the one for Big Bob's Auto Barn.

29

And Now, More *Pottymouth and Stoopid!*

"**I**s that supposed to be me?" said Anna as a character who looked like her cartoon twin flitted across the TV carrying a stack of encyclopedias.

Pottymouth entered the scene from the other side of the screen.

Here are some real words I found for you, Pottymouth:

bumfuzzle, cattywampus, taradiddle, and snickersnee.

Sludgepuggle!

"Do you know why they call you Pottymouth?" said Anna Britannica. Her cartoon talked through its nose and made her sound like a total nerd.

Pottymouth shrugged. "Because they're all a bunch of boomboolly bumbuzzlers?"

"Perhaps," said Anna. "But most likely because you are given to the frequent use of vulgar language."

"Oh. Why do they call Stoopid 'Stoopid'?"

"Because he is."

As Pottymouth and the Anna character laughed meanly, she slid offscreen. (Her part was kind of small in the show. Anna was lucky.)

Next, Pottymouth snuck into the empty school office (accompanied by sneaky piano key plinks) and grabbed hold of the PA microphone.

The camera moved in for a close-up.

I think the actor playing Pottymouth was the same guy who did the voice for the Principal Blerguson character, because Pottymouth's imitation of the principal was dead-on perfect (even better than Michael's Principal Ferguson impersonation in real life).

"Greetings, greezspittle students and floofilating faculty, this is Principal Blerguson, your head dorkalodoofus, speaking. The authorities have advised me that zombies from Mars have just landed behind the school. They are not here to learn. They are here to eat your brains. You are, therefore, dismissed for the day. Kindly evacuate your classrooms and cover your ears, kids, because that's where Martian zombies like to stick their brain-sucking straws. Have a nice day, you flufferknuckles!"

Stoopid came running into the scene, chased by the slow-moving Mrs. Toothface.

"Woo-hoo!" shouted Stoopid. "School's out!"

"Run, you flufferknuckles!" cried Pottymouth. "Run!"

While Pottymouth and Stoopid attempted to

slap each other a high-five (Stoopid missed), dozens of panicked, screeching cartoon kids streamed out of classroom doors.

Principal Blerguson, with a whole roll of toilet paper stuck to his shoe, came running out of the staff bathroom, the roll trailing behind him. Mrs. Toothface slipped on a banana peel, landed on her bottom, and bounced down the hall like a runaway tennis ball, crying, "Oh my! Oh my!" the whole way.

While the panicked mob fled from the school, Pottymouth and Stoopid casually strolled along the sidewalk.

"So, what do you want to do now?" asked Pottymouth.

"I dunno," said Stoopid. "Maybe play electric-skateboardball?"

"Hicklesnicklepox! That sounds awesome!"

And the show ended with Stoopid racing across the driveway on a really fast motorized skateboard, tossing up his shot, and, of course, slamming into the garage door.

Again.

The closing credits started to roll.

We snapped off the TV.

And sat there staring at the screen for like an hour.

School Dazed and Confused

When Michael and I headed back to school, we didn't know what to expect.

Would the *Pottymouth & Stoopid* show turn us into celebrities?

Would we, all of a sudden, be famous?

Would everybody want our autographs?

Would people stop throwing Tater Tots at us in the cafeteria?

The answer was no, no, no, and no such luck.

The next day, we were, basically, walking, talking insult piñatas.

Everybody lined up to take a potshot at us. It seemed a lot of our fellow middle-grade students had tuned into the Cartoon Factory at eight o'clock, just like we had. The ones who'd missed

it watched it on YouTube as soon as they could. So by the time Michael and I came to school, pretty much everyone had seen it.

"So, *Stoopid*," said this guy named Kenny Gregg, "was that cartoon supposed to be you?"

"I dunno," I mumbled.

"Well, he looked like you, he acted like you, and he sure was stupid like you."

"No," I said. "He was stupider."

"Maybe. So, I have to ask you one question: Does your face hurt from slamming into the garage door?"

"It's a cartoon, Kenny," I explained. "Cartoons slam into walls all the time."

Kenny nodded. "And they never get hurt. What's up with that?"

"I don't know."

"Are you going to blow up or something next week? Because when cartoon characters explode, they come back looking fine. Are you going to blow up?"

"How should I know?" This might have been the dumbest conversation I'd ever had.

"So how come the Cartoon Factory did a whole TV show about you?"

I shrugged. Michael had people coming up to him and asking the same kind of questions, including that girl Emma—the one with the braces.

You called me a flufferknuckle in real life before it was on TV.

Do I get money for that?

"So, are you, like, the *real* Pottymouth?" Emma asked.

"My name is Michael."

"Riiiight. But everybody calls you Pottymouth, remember?"

"Yeah. How could I possipoopily forget?"

"See? There you go, pottymouthing again. I am so confused. How is it even possible that someone would want to base a cartoon character on, you know, *you?*"

Michael just shrugged, but Emma kept rattling away, flashing her steel teeth.

"I mean, I can see why they wanted to make a cartoon about the real SpongeBob. He lives in a pineapple at the bottom of the sea. That's interesting. But why would they waste their time

making *you* famous? It's not like you're anything special.

"You're nobody," said Emma. "All you do is invent words that don't make any sense. Making a cartoon about you would just be stupid. No, wait. Stoopid's the other guy."

"Emma?" said Michael. "Nothing personal, but sometimes you sound like a dorkalodoofus."

"Oh, really? Because that's what Pottymouth said about Principal Blerguson. You stole that joke from Pottymouth! The one on TV."

"No. The cartoon dude stole it from *me*."

Emma propped her hands on her hips. "Who would do something as idiotic as stealing words from you?"

That was the zillion-dollar question.

If the characters on the TV show were, somehow, based on me and Michael (and let's face it, it would be a crazy coincidence if they weren't), who was responsible?

And why?

We were as confused as everybody else.

Somebody we knew had taken the worst stuff from our lives and turned it into slapstick comedy for a TV show.

And hadn't even bothered to tell us about it.

FRED GRABOWSKI

Pottymouth & Stoopid's Biggest Fan

I love this show.

I've seen every episode. Six times!

Remember when Pottymouth tricked Principal Blerguson into celebrating National Boogerschnizzle Day?

That was so hicklepicklepoxing hysterical.

I bet you Pottymouth is the one who came up with Mrs. Toothface's name because it is sooooo perfect.

And Stoopid? You have to be pretty smart to

try some of the dumb stuff he does. Brave too.
I love both these guys. Why? I don't know.
Maybe because they remind me of me!

Things Continue to Suck Weasel Eggs

G ym class was the worst.

Even Coach Ball had seen *Pottymouth & Stoopid* on Cartoon Factory.

"So do you two kids know the guys who write that cartoon?" he asked us while he pounded a basketball on the hardwood floor. Repeatedly. "Because, I've got to be honest with you, that Stoopid kid reminded me of you, Mr. Scungili."

Yeah, that's something else my ex-dad gave me. A skeevy last name.

"Do you still play basketball on your skateboard?" Coach Ball asked.

"Sometimes," I mumbled.

"You ever slam into the wall like Stoopid does all the time on TV?"

"Once."

"That's what made him so stupid," snickered a jock named Luke Lucas. "The dumdum banged his skull against a brick wall too many times and dented his brain."

Everybody in gym class cracked up, including Coach Ball.

"That's pretty funny, Mr. Lucas," he said. "Hey, Stoopid—"

"That's not my name," I mumbled.

"Huh?"

"Nothing."

"You should call up the knuckleheads at the Cartoon Factory. Tell them to put that line about how you became a dumdum in one of your shows."

"It's not my show," I mumbled.

"I'll do it," said Luke. "I'll sell them my joke. TV-show writers get paid a ton of money. The only hard part of the job is getting those tiny little cartoon people to memorize all their lines. They have to rehearse like six hours a day."

Just so you know, Luke Lucas always acts like he knows what he's talking about even when he doesn't. *Especially* when he doesn't.

"If the cartoons don't memorize their lines in time, they get erased."

Yep. This was from one of the guys who always called *me* stupid. Listening to Luke Lucas, I had to wonder if maybe *he* was the inspiration for the cartoon character Stoopid. Not that I would ever say that. When you've been made fun of your whole life, you have a hard time making fun of other people because you know how it feels. I think they call that empathy. (I'd ask my teacher, but she already thinks I'm an idiot.)

After school, everybody wanted to see Michael and me do the moronic stunts that Pottymouth and Stoopid did on their TV show—especially the one where the cartoon Stoopid dunked a

basketball without letting go of the ball. His whole body squeezed through the hoop and then the net like a Slurpee going through a straw.

"Do it, Stoopid!" somebody shouted as a mob clustered around us under the basketball hoops on the playground. "Just like on TV!"

"Don't just stand there like a flufferknuckle, Pottymouth," shouted somebody else. "Toss Stoopid up in the air like you did on the show!"

"And scream 'Hicklesnicklepox!' when you give him the heave-ho," added Emma, who had pushed her way to the front of the crowd. "Because when cartoon you said it, I just about died laughing!"

Michael and I looked at each other and shrugged. After a whole day of nonstop Pottymouth-and-Stoopid-ness, we didn't have much choice. Our best defense was a good offense, whatever that means. (It's something coaches and jocks say all the time, but, to be honest, I've always thought the best defense was a moat. Or maybe an army of bodyguards.)

Plus, this could be our best shot ever at making

good names for ourselves with the other kids. Names that didn't involve Pottymouth *or* Stoopid.

Anyway, Michael and I started imitating the characters from the TV show.

"Hey, Pottymouth," I said to Michael. "I have another amazingly genius idea. The five-point shot!"

I was quoting from the TV show. Michael and I had watched the thing like eighteen times online as we tried to figure out who knew all those details about our lives. Was it the teachers at school? Did they all have side jobs as writers for the Cartoon Factory?

"What's a five-point shot, Stoopid?" asked Michael, delivering the next line from the show perfectly. He put a confounded look on his face, since three is the highest number of points for a single shot in basketball. "How can anybody score that many pumpadillio points?"

"Easy," I said. "If I get the ball *plus* all four of my limbs through the hoop, I score five points!"

"Does your head count too?" asked Michael, the same way Pottymouth did on TV.

"Uh, yeah," I said, doing my dead-on Stoopid voice. "So I guess my five-point shot is really a six-point shot."

"Unless you count your fingers and toes," said Michael. "Then it's a twenty-one-point shot."

I rapped my knuckles against my head the way Stoopid did in the TV show.

"Too much math." I moaned in mock agony. "My head hurts."

"Just wait," said Michael, "we haven't even shoved it through the hicklepickle hoop yet..."

Yep. We thought we sounded exactly like the cartoon characters, but the other kids didn't seem to agree.

"*Lame,*" groaned Emma. "You suck at being Pottymouth and Stoopid."

"You suck at being *you!*" added Luke Lucas.

And the whole crowd walked away.

Michael never even got a chance to shout "Hicklesnicklepox!" or shove me through the hoop and net.

That was probably a good thing.

TONY SCUNGILI

David's "Ex-Dad"

The day after *Pottymouth & Stoopid* debuted, I swung by the offices of the Cartoon Factory.

They gave me a standing ovation!

Seriously.

Everybody stood up at their desks and started clapping.

Somebody popped open a bottle of bubbly.

Several attractive young ladies started flirting with me.

"We just got the numbers for the show," said the head of the network.

That meant he'd seen the overnight ratings.

"Is the show a hit?" I asked, figuring it probably was or the pretty girls would've kept the champagne chilling in the back of the fridge.

"A hit?" said the network bigwig. "It's a home run!"

I shouted, "Hicklesnicklepox!"

Porter Malkiel, the president and chief executive officer of Cartoon Factory Inc., called me a "grizzlegoober genius"!

I went right out and bought myself a new sports car. A cherry-red convertible.

This show is the best thing to ever happen to me.

My new girlfriend agrees.

She's totally gorgeous, with great hair that looks amazing blowing in the breeze when I drop the top down on my shiny new convertible.

I have lots of other friends too.

They're all very sincerely happy for me.

Everyone loves it when we go out and I pay

for all the food and drinks they want. We all have a great time!

I knew that one day, I would smell like Success.

That's the name of this new cologne I bought. It costs one thousand dollars an ounce.

Guess what?

Thanks to *Pottymouth & Stoopid,* I can buy it by the gallon!

Do Pottymouth and
Stoopid for Us!

My ex-dad never followed up on that promise to pay Mom all the child support he owed her. In fact, after the lunch at McDonald's, we didn't hear from him again.

Big surprise.

So, while we waited for the court to send him another reminder, she hauled Michael and me to school in her old clunker of a car.

"Remember, guys," she said every morning when she dropped us off, "what people say about you says more about them than it does about you."

Yeah. Right.

Like we were ever going to believe *that*.

After a few weeks' worth of *Pottymouth & Stoopid* episodes, everybody at school was imitating us. I mean, they were imitating the cartoon

characters who were imitating us. And, like always, they thought they were way better.

People started wearing T-shirts with Michael's words printed on the chest: *Flufferknuckle. Hicklesnicklepox. Snifflepiggle.*

But when Michael made up a new word, one that wasn't from the TV show, watch out! Girls laughed at him. Boys called him mental. Teachers pulled out their detention slips.

"That's just gross," said a girl when Michael said *flurrzlegerkin* for the first time in science class. (He'd just discovered what happened when you mixed three kinds of clear chemicals together—they turned colors!)

Meanwhile, she was wearing a T-shirt with *Snifflepiggle* splashed all over the front in a starburst. Guess who made up *that* word.

Yeah.

Stoopid inspired T-shirts too. The big seller was one that said *I'm with Stoopid.* It had a finger pointing up— at the person wearing it.

Lunchtime in the cafeteria became feeding time at the zoo for Pottymouth and Stoopid. Everybody came over to either gawk at us or make fun of us.

"Do something stupid," they'd say to me.

"Put a french fry in your ear!"

"Put a hamburger bun on your head like it's a hat!"

"Juggle your Jell-O cubes!"

One day, I got so mad at the Stoopid ideas that I slammed my fist down on the table to make everyone shut up. I slammed it *hard*.

Dumb move.

My fist hit the handle of my fork, which was sitting in a bowl of macaroni and cheese. The fork became a catapult. The mac and cheese became a projectile that rivaled the flaming catapult missiles they flung in castle sieges. Mine landed with a splat.

On top of Coach Ball's head.

I'm going to be running laps around the gym for the rest of my life.

Kids tormented Michael whenever he walked down the hall. They'd tip his books out of his arms, throw paper balls at his head, and trip him by stepping on his shoelaces—anything to make him go ballistic and let loose with a string of classic Pottymouth words.

Luckily for Anna, nobody bothered her too much.

"She's just a nerd on the show," they'd say. "She's not even funny."

By week six, Anna Britannica had stopped showing up on the *Pottymouth & Stoopid* show. Her catchphrase was *Brain power. Use it or lose it,* but it hadn't caught on. It just wasn't dumb enough.

Through it all, Michael and I never, ever went whining to anyone. We're just not whiners. When life throws curveballs at us, we duck.

But when we were alone, up in our tree house after another day of being the original Pottymouth and Stoopid, we'd let our real feelings bubble up.

"We didn't do anything to deserve this," I said.

"We didn't fudging ask for this," said Michael.

"Somebody must've spied on us and turned our entire lives into one dumb TV show," I said, because we still didn't know who had done this to us.

"This is so wrong," said Anna, climbing up to join us. "In so many ways."

"It's unfair," I declared. "School is unfair. TV is unfair. *Life* is unfair."

"And TV used to be our friend," added Michael. "Sludgepuggle."

"Everything in the whole entire universe is unfair!" I said, slamming my fist down hard.

I have to stop doing that. Because this time, I banged a hole in our tree-house floor. It was pretty wide, so I covered it up with a sheet of cardboard.

But then, two minutes later, I forgot I had just punched a hole in the floor and I stepped on the cardboard.

Oops!

One leg went all the way through. The other didn't. That'll hurt.

Yes, it was a stupid move. But like I said before, doing stupid stuff doesn't automatically mean I'm Stoopid.

It just means I'm a kid.

33

Principal Blerguson

After episode seven of *Pottymouth & Stoopid* aired on the Cartoon Factory channel, Michael and I were summoned to Principal Ferguson's office.

"Do you think he wants you to autograph his schnizzleflicking *I'm with Stoopid* T-shirt?" Michael asked me.

"I doubt it. He probably wants to hear you say *Skifferdeejibberdee*."

"Pottymouth says it wrong on TV," said Michael.

"I know."

"The cartoon dude never seems really angry. *Skifferdeejibberdee* is a level-nine word. I say it only when *sludgepuggle* just isn't strong enough."

Mrs. Tuttafacio, the school secretary, told us to sit down and wait.

She also gave us a super-dirty look. I had a feeling she had seen Mrs. Toothface on the *Pottymouth & Stoopid* show and probably assumed we were the ones who'd told the cartoonists to draw her that way, since everybody—students, teachers, *and* the school administrators—called us Pottymouth and Stoopid. They figured Michael and I had some kind of "technical adviser" jobs at the Cartoon Factory, giving the joke writers ideas about people to make fun of.

We didn't. If we had, we wouldn't have let them make so much fun of *us*. Not that anyone believed us when we said that.

Anyway, we couldn't apologize to Mrs. Tuttafacio. If we did, it would be like we were admitting we were the ones who'd called her Toothface.

She waddled down the corridor to Principal

Ferguson's office and rapped on the door.

We heard someone grunt. "Send them in. Now!"

"Principal Ferguson will see you now," Mrs. Tuttafacio announced majestically. She had a huge grin on her face, like she was looking forward to seeing our heads chopped off in the village square.

Michael and I shuffled up the hall and stepped into the principal's office. It was pretty nice. He had a bookcase *and* a carpet.

Principal Ferguson didn't waste any time letting us know why we were in his office.

"What is the meaning of this?" he demanded, pointing at his computer screen.

On it was a freeze-frame from the most recent episode of *Pottymouth & Stoopid*.

"Oh," I said. "That's Principal Blerguson."

"I know who he is," said Principal Ferguson whose name (duh) sounded a lot like the name of the principal in the cartoon show. "What I want to know is why this character's name is so similar to mine."

"We don't know why they called him that, sir," said Michael.

"We had nothing to do with anything on that show," I added.

"A likely story," said Principal Ferguson. "After all, you *are* Pottymouth and Stoopid."

"Don't call us that!" said Michael, then he bit

his tongue to stop himself from telling Principal Ferguson he was a flufferknuckle.

The principal glared at us and clicked the Play button.

You need to loosen up, Principal Blerguson.

I can't! My underpants are so tight, they're riding up my butt worse than the school superintendent!

On-screen, Stoopid said, "When my underpants are too tight, I cut the elastic. No more wedgies!"

"So you ruin your own underwear?" said

Principal Blerguson. "That's just stupid!"

"That's my name," said Stoopid. "Don't wear it out!"

"You're a bunchybutt swizzlenizzle," said Pottymouth.

"What's that supposed to mean?" asked Principal Blerguson.

"It means you need a new pair of underpants, sir," said Pottymouth.

"Would you like to borrow a pair of mine?" said Stoopid. "I have some in my locker. They're not new, but I wore them for only like a day or two so they're not too dirty."

"Could you be any grosser?" the cartoon principal yelled.

Stoopid kept going. "I forgot to take them home so my mom could wash them. She puts them in the dishwasher, but only on the bottom rack. Because they're *under*pants."

The laugh track on the show got really loud; it sounded like the whole audience was cracking up. That's how they make jokes on TV seem funny even when they're not.

Principal Ferguson snapped off the video. "How dare you!" he snarled at us.

"Um, how dare us what, sir?" I asked.

"How dare you make fun of me like that on national television?"

"We didn't do it," said Michael.

"Don't lie to me, son. Why else would this cartoon principal be called Blerguson?"

"It wasn't us!" I said. "We don't write TV shows. We barely have time to write essays for English class."

Principal Ferguson crossed his arms over his chest. "Nonsense. You two reprobates are responsible for sullying my reputation."

"No, we're not," I said.

"We don't even know what *reprobates* and *sullying* mean!" said Michael.

Principal Ferguson stared at us. Then he scowled. Then he pulled out two thick manila folders.

Uh-oh.

Our permanent records!

34

Blerguson's Big Surprise

ver since first grade, teachers had warned Michael and me that if we did something really bad, it would end up in our permanent records.

The way they talked about it, your permanent record followed you around your entire life, from pre-K to middle school to high school to college and even after that. If you applied for a job, the guy interviewing you could look at your permanent record and say, "We'd love to hire you, David, but we see that you picked your nose in first grade. Sorry, it's the unemployment line for you."

"Do you boys know what these are?" asked Principal Ferguson, tapping the two folders.

Michael and I gasped at the same time. We'd never seen our permanent records before.

"Everything you've ever done, the good and the bad—or, in your cases, just the bad—is in here. Until today, I saw no reason to dig any deeper into who you two boys were because, frankly, I already *knew* who you were: another pair of losers. Let's face it, neither one of you is ever going to find a cure for cancer or become president of the United States."

"I might," snapped Michael. "I might do both."

"Riiiight," said Principal Ferguson, who was reminding me more and more of Principal Blerguson from the cartoon. "Like *that's* ever going to happen."

"It could," said Michael.

"When pigs fly," muttered the principal as he flipped through the pages stuffed into our folders.

"They do," I said. "There's a movie coming out—"

"Life isn't a movie, young man. Or a cartoon show."

One of the papers in my folder seemed to stop him in his tracks.

"Which one of you is David?" he asked, sounding sort of shocked.

"Me," I said. "I'm the one they call Stoopid."

"Well, they're wrong."

"Huh?"

"Do you remember taking an IQ test, Mr. Scungili?"

"Vaguely," I said. "When I was little. It was supposed to measure our intelligence quotients."

"That's right," said Principal Ferguson, still sounding like he was astounded by something in my permanent record. He even forgot to be mean and nasty to us. "Did you know you have an IQ of 159?"

"No," I said. "Is that good?"

"It's better than good, David," a shocked Principal Ferguson said, "an IQ of 150 or above means you are highly intelligent. A *genius*."

I couldn't believe my ears. "I'm not stupid?"

The principal shook his head. "No, you're not, David. Neither is Michael."

"Seriously?" said Michael.

"Your IQ is 160."

"Whoa. I'm smarter than David?"

"Slightly."

"I guess that's why he comes up with all those

cool new words," I said. "He's too smart to stick with the ordinary ones."

Principal Ferguson leaned back in his chair. Studied us.

"So, tell me, boys: What's up with this Pottymouth and Stoopid act? Is this something you two cooked up years ago to hide your true potential?"

"No, sir," I said. "They're not really nicknames we'd pick out for ourselves."

"In fact," said Michael, "we had nothing to do with it. Other flufferknuckles came up with those names for us when we were in preschool, and they just stuck."

We just didn't know which one of those flufferknuckles had put us on TV!

35

Our New Homework
Assignment

Do you know how often the Cartoon Factory
plays reruns of *Pottymouth & Stoopid*?
Every day. *All* day.

Michael and I could watch our cartoon twins smash into walls, sit on wet paint, and say "Sludge-puggle!" at least six or seven times a day—more if we stayed up past one o'clock in the morning.

Instead of making us cooler, the show made us even more miserable than before. Mom told the school we were sick and let us stay home, and she even called in sick herself so she could try to make us feel better.

"I baked you boys some chocolate chip cookies," she announced. "I used your grandpa's recipe, David."

That was really sweet. So were the cookies. She used way too much sugar. (I don't think Grandpa ever actually followed a recipe; he just sort of tossed the right amounts of ingredients into the bowl out of instinct.)

Michael and I pretended to enjoy Mom's cookies, but when she wasn't looking, we slid them off the table so the dog could eat them—even though we don't have a dog.

"I have an idea," said Mom later as she vacuumed cookie crumbs off the floor. "Why don't you boys do some research? Find out who's making fun of you on national TV."

She might not have baked good cookies, but Mom had come up with an excellent idea.

And so began our biggest homework assignment ever.

The first thing we did was pause the end credits of the *Pottymouth & Stoopid* show.

There were two problems.

One, the list of names of people who worked on the show was super-small and sort of shoved over to one side of the screen.

The other problem?

When we finally dug up a magnifying glass and read the *created by* and *written by* credits, they didn't even sound real. They said the show was *created by Charles D. Chucklepuss* and *written by the usual gang of knuckleheads.*

That's just how the Cartoon Factory rolls. Everything is a joke to them, including our lives.

So we tried a more direct approach.

We Googled like maniacs and finally found

the phone number for the Cartoon Factory head-quarters in Chicago.

At first, we couldn't get through. Our call was answered by one of those robo-machines that asks you to keep pushing buttons until your fingers bleed.

- To order Pottymouth and Stoopid merchandise, press one.
- To complain about something Pottymouth said, press two.
- To sue us because you did something stupid after you saw Stoopid do it, type "good luck with that" on your keypad.
- To speak to a human being, hang up the phone, go outside, and wait for the mailman. He might be interested in a friendly conversation.

"Frizzlegristle hicklesnicklepox!" said Michael after like two hours of telephone-button pushing that led nowhere.

I had another idea.

We Googled the president and CEO of the Cartoon Factory, a guy named Porter Malkiel.

We found a few video clips of him talking to advertising executives. Michael replayed the clips like a million times so he could get the Cartoon Factory big cheese's voice down cold. And then we called this other number we found on the business page for the Cartoon Factory.

"Hello," said Michael, "this is Porter Malkiel, your president and chief executive officer, speaking."

"Yes, *sir,* sir," said the eager dude on the other end of the phone. "How may I direct your call, sir?"

"I want to talk to whoever is in charge of *Pottymouth and Stoopid.*"

"You mean the brand-new program that's the biggest hit this network has had in years?"

"Yes. Who's in charge of it?"

The dude on the other end of the line was silent. For like five seconds. Finally he said, not nearly so eagerly, "That would be you, Mr. Malkiel."

I grabbed the phone out of Michael's hand. "We're the real Pottymouth and Stoopid!" I shouted into it.

And the guy at the Cartoon Factory hung up on me.

36

The Un-Wanted Posters

Since we couldn't call in sick forever, we headed back to school the next day.

Big mistake.

The homemade posters didn't make much sense.

Until Kaya Kennecky came along and explained them to us. (She also had a fresh stack of posters printed on pink paper tucked under her arm.)

"You two doofuses are ruining everybody's favorite TV show!"

"Oh, really?" I asked. "How does that work?"

"Pottymouth and Stoopid on TV are funny. You two in real life are just lousy lamebrains."

"And you're a flufferknuckle," said Michael.

"See?" screeched Kaya. "You don't even say it right! It's *fluf*-fer-*knuck*-le! You're a bad Pottymouth, Pottymouth. Stop pretending to be someone you're not, Michael."

"Wait—you know my name?"

"We asked at the office. Mrs. Toothface—I mean Tuttafacio—looked it up on the computer. It took her like fifteen minutes."

"She didn't know our real names either?" I asked.

"Of course not, David. Why should she waste

her time on something as unimportant as your lame-o name-o's? She has bus schedules to organize."

"You know I'm David?"

"No. I know you're nobodies faking that you're the real Pottymouth and Stoopid. Well, *Michael and David,* quit causing trouble. You're probably trying to sue the Cartoon Factory for stealing your names. I'm not going to stand by and let you ruin the best show on TV!"

"Uh, *you're* the one who stuck us with these nicknames back in preschool, Kaya," I pointed out. "You've been calling us Pottymouth and Stoopid for eight years now. So how are *we* the fakers when the show just started a few days ago?"

"Sludgepuggle," mumbled Michael in agreement.

Kaya stomped her left foot hard. "Stop! Doing! That! We love *Pottymouth and Stoopid,* the TV show. It's you two we can't stand!"

She huffed away and started taping up more posters.

The funny part was, Kaya was on the show

too, only she didn't know it. There was a hilariously bratty character called Kara Kentucky who followed Pottymouth and Stoopid around and tortured them with pranks and name-calling. I guess Kaya didn't realize that she was the inspiration for Kara, because if she knew, she wouldn't have loved the show so much.

Our friend Anna came up behind us.

"Don't worry, you guys," she said. "There are more of us than there are of her."

"Huh?" I said.

"There can be only one middle-school princess," said Anna, gesturing toward Kaya. "But there will always be a million peasants."

"So we're doomed to be pippleskreeking peasants?" said Michael.

"It's a metaphor," said Anna. "Work with me."

The class change bell rang. Fred Grabowski and Will Hunt came out of a classroom and headed right for us.

"There they are!" said Fred.

"The real deal!" said Will.

"Huh?" I said again, looking around to see

who they were talking about. (For a guy with a super-high IQ, I was having a lot of trouble with my vocabulary words that day.)

"Pottymouth and Stoopid," said Fred. "They're just like us. Kind of dorky, kind of klutzy."

"Kind of awesometastic!" said Will.

Then I noticed he was wearing an *Awesometastic* T-shirt. Pottymouth and Stoopid said that on TV all the time.

"Way to stick up for the underdogs, guys!" said Fred, fist-bumping us. "Way to represent!"

"But," said Michael, "we didn't represent anything."

"Yeah, right," said Fred.

"You guys are like heroes," said Will.

Then they wanted to take selfies with us. So did about twenty kids who lined up behind them.

We may never be prom kings and queens, but Pottymouth and Stoopid have made us superstars!
AWESOMETASTIC

We're Going Global!

That evening, Mom called me into the living room to check out the nightly news. "Quick!" she shouted.

"What is it?" I asked, zooming over.

"You won't believe this," she said, pointing at the screen.

"It has quickly become one of the biggest hits in cable-TV history," said the anchorman, who had bouffy hair that looked like a hat. "Not just here in America, where teenagers mimic everything Pottymouth and Stoopid say or do, but all across the globe. In China, millions tune in every night to catch the antics of *Biànpén Kǒu Bèn*. In Germany, they're *Potty Mund und Dumm*. And in France, kids love *Bouche Fétide et Stupide*.

"With us tonight, the brains behind the number-one hit on TV."

The camera angle shifted and there he was.

Ex-Dad.

His black hair (what little he had left) was slicked back and gelled into place. He was dressed in a slick black suit and wore an even slicker diamond-encrusted black watch on his wrist. Everything about him was slick and black. He looked like a well-dressed oil spill.

"It was him," Mom and I muttered at exactly the same time.

"This explains everything," said Mom.

"Yeah," I said. "Remind me never to go to the McDonald's with Ex-Dad again."

"So, Tony," said the anchorman, "how'd you come up with this incredibly fresh and original

idea to make two lovable losers the stars of a cartoon?"

"Hard to say, Biff," said Ex-Dad, pretending to be modest. "But I've been an idea guy my whole life. I used to work in advertising and I have a couple novels being bid on by major New York City publishers. Hollywood's even calling me about doing a *Pottymouth and Stoopid* movie deal. For me, Biff, ideas are like lightning bolts. You just have to know how to catch them before they disappear." He mimed snagging something out of the air. "It also helps if you're wearing rubber-soled shoes so you don't get electrocuted."

"Was there an inspiration for your two main characters?" asked Biff. "Are Pottymouth and Stoopid based on people you remember from your own days in middle school?"

"Nope. They're based on two modern-day middle-schoolers. My son, David, is Stoopid. His best friend, Michael, is Pottymouth."

The anchorman's jaw dropped. "Seriously?" he said. "You're making fun of your own son on TV?"

Ex-Dad smirked. "We're not making fun of him, Biff. We're making him *famous!*"

"Do your son and his best friend receive any kind of financial compensation from you or the Cartoon Factory?"

"You mean, are they being paid?"

"That's right."

Ex-Dad blinked. Several times. "Next question, Biff."

Mom snapped off the TV.

"The answer is no, Biff!" she said to the blank screen. "They haven't gotten anything from *Pottymouth and Stoopid!*"

That wasn't completely correct. So far, the show had given us a whole lot of grief.

Pottymouth and Stoopid Make the News!

"It's not true!" Kaya Kennecky screamed in our faces the next day at school. "What that guy said on TV last night was a total lie!"

"You're probably right," I told her. "No way has my ex-dad ever written a whole novel."

"Novels have a ton of wooflewacking words in them," added Michael.

"That's not what I meant!" screeched Kaya, stomping her foot. "He's probably not even your dad. No way are Pottymouth and Stoopid based on you two losers."

"David and Michael were merely the proto-types, Kaya," said our biggest fan, Fred Grabowski, who was sort of following us around everywhere like a puppy dog. "Stand-ins, if you will, for the invisible multitude who make up the vast major-ity of middle-schoolers. In a way, we are all Pottymouth and Stoopid."

The spirit of Pottymouth and Stoopid embiggens all of us, though we dare not speak of it, for thou shalt make fun of us if we do!

Fred can get pretty goofy when he makes his grand pronouncements. He even sticks his finger in the air like he's the Jebediah Springfield statue on *The Simpsons.*

When we got home from school, there were all sorts of TV trucks with satellite dishes mounted on their roofs parked outside our house. There was also an army of camera crews and TV reporters camped out on our lawn.

"There they are!" shouted one as we started walking to the front door. "The real Pottymouth and Stoopid!"

"Bouche Fétide et Stupide!" screamed a reporter wearing a beret. *"Bouche Fétide et Stupide!"*

Three dozen cameras were aimed at us. Three dozen microphones were thrust in our faces.

"David and Michael?" said the man with the bouffy hair who had interviewed Ex-Dad the night before. "Biff Bilgewater here. How does it feel to have the whole world laughing at you?"

"W-well, uh," I stammered. "I guess everybody needs a good laugh now and then. They say

laughter is the best medicine. Except it doesn't really work on zits."

Okay, that was dumb. But I was nervous.

I'd also just made a big mistake. Since I was the one who'd actually spoken, all the cameras and microphones zoomed in on me.

"David?" asked a female reporter. "What's it like being called stupid in dozens of foreign languages?"

"I dunno..."

"In Czech, you're Hloupý. In the Philippines, you're Tanga. In Mexico, you're Estúpido."

"And here in America," said Biff Bilgewater, "you're just plain Stoopid."

And that's when Michael exploded—the same way he did when Mr. Chaffapopoulos was our substitute teacher.

"Rrrrrggghhh, hicklesnicklepox! David isn't stupid, you flufferknuckles. He's my friend, and he's a genius, so stick your grizzlenoogies in your boomboolies and leave him alone."

Mom came racing out of the house with a huge golf umbrella. "Hide behind this, boys."

She used that umbrella like a shield to block the TV cameras so they couldn't get any more video footage of us. Then she turned it into a battering ram to part the crowd. Michael and I followed her up our cracked-concrete path and into the house.

When the front door closed behind us, we were finally safe.

Mom lowered the huge umbrella.

"Uh-oh," said Michael. "Who are all *these* flufferknuckles?"

Yep. The living room was even more crowded than the front lawn.

39

Fan Club Fail

The house was filled with relatives (most of whom I didn't even know we had), Mom's friends from work, and a few neighbors (I didn't know we had those either).

Anna, Fred, and Will were there too. So was a kid named Katherine Kelly who didn't even go to our school but who was friends with Fred Grabowski from chess camp.

"They kept bugging me to bring them," Anna explained.

"So this is where you guys come up with your

awesometastic ideas," said Will, looking around.

"Nice wallpaper," added Fred.

"I don't know you guys, but I love you," said Katherine.

"Hicklesnicklepox," grumbled Michael.

"Yeah," said Fred. "I know what you mean. It's a circus out there."

"It sort of looks like one in here too," I said.

"What's everybody doing here?" I finally asked Mom.

"They all heard the news. That you-know-who and you-know-who-else are based on Michael and you. They're your friends and supporters."

"And there's a new episode on tonight!" said a guy in a grease-spattered apron who, I guess, was a cook at the restaurant where Mom waitressed. "Eight o'clock." He pulled out his phone and scrolled down the screen. "It's called 'Science Fair or Unfair?' Sounds hysterical. Do you guys know what happens in it?"

I had a hunch but I played dumb because, well, that's what Stoopid is supposed to do, right?

"We don't have a clue," I said.

"I bet it's about when you guys did those awesome chili-cheese corn dogs and the Zip Tray!" said Fred.

"That was so cool!" said Will. "Best science project ever!"

"It was a disaster," I reminded them.

"A megagloppolis mess," added Michael.

"Only because Kaya Kennecky and all the popular kids sabotaged you guys," said Fred.

"Seriously," said Anna, who'd been part of that project too.

"If only the school had implemented your suggested reforms." Fred sighed. "You three were simply ahead of your time."

"Someday," said Katherine, "maybe the rest of the world will catch up with you."

Wow. I had never thought about it like that.

So we went ahead and enjoyed the party, the pizza, and the soda (after lowering all the window shades so the TV people out on the lawn couldn't snoop).

At eight o'clock on the dot, we heard the familiar theme song bubbling out of the TV.

In the first scene, Pottymouth whipped up a batch of "chilitastic, cheese-o-mastic, corn-dog dookle sticks" and Stoopid tried to jam one up his nose because it smelled so good.

The crowd in front of the TV were laughing their heads off. Well, everyone except me and Michael.

I didn't know what was weirder—our fans, or the fact that we had any.

40

Taking Out the Trash

The next morning, the phone started ringing around six.

Every *Wake Up America*- and *Have a Good Day Today*-type TV show had producers calling to see if Michael and I would do interviews.

"If you have a camera in your laptop," said one, "we could put you on the air, live, right now!"

"Um, I don't have a laptop."

"No problem. We could do it over your cell phone."

"My cell phone doesn't have a camera in it."

"Really?"

"Yeah. It's an antique."

"You're the star of the TV show that's number one in half the world and you can't afford a laptop or an iPhone?"

"I'm not the...oh, never mind."

One thing I could do perfectly with my old-fashioned phone was hang up on people. Which I did. Repeatedly. For like an hour.

Meanwhile, Mom kept hanging up on people on the landline. Finally, she just yanked the wire out of the wall. I slid the battery out of my cell phone. Amazingly, we didn't get any more calls from the TV producers after that.

"Let's hustle, hon," she said, checking her watch. "You need to be at school and I need to open the restaurant. Can you haul out the recycling and grab the newspaper?"

"On it."

I headed for the front door lugging a clear plastic bag loaded with soda cans and brown bottles from our *Pottymouth & Stoopid* viewing party.

When I stepped out on the front porch, I smiled.

All the TV people were gone. Thanks to them, our grass wouldn't need to be mowed for weeks. They had trampled it flat.

I went to the curb, tossed my recycling bag into the green bin, and then bent down to pick up the newspaper.

I froze in mid-bend.

There was a banner headline screaming across the front page. Beneath it was a pair of photographs. The ones Michael and I had taken last year for the middle-school yearbook. We both had our eyes closed but nobody had cared enough to do a reshoot.

Good thing we have a paper-recycling bin too.

I picked up the newspaper and tossed it on top of the stack of crumpled cardboard and junk mail.

An elderly lady walking her froufrou dog down the sidewalk didn't like that.

"What do you think you're doing? The printed word is precious. Words are not to be casually discarded, young man. You probably don't even know how to read. All you know how to do is play those video games. Mark my words, video games will make you stupid."

"Yeah," I said. "So will everything else around here."

41

School's Out... Forever

Mom and I swung by Michael's house to pick him up like we did most mornings. His front lawn was trampled too.

For the first time since forever, Michael's foster parents, Mr. and Mrs. Brawley, were waiting with him at the end of the driveway.

"There she is!" screamed Mrs. Brawley. "The stupid #$%^* who married that @#$%£ thief Scungili! Your ex-husband is making a %$#@ ton of money off our #%$^#@ beloved foster son."

"We want our #$%& cut!" shouted Mr. Brawley.

"We demand a %^#$ royalty. Fifteen £¢&% per-cent!"

"Don't be an &#$%, Morris!" shrieked Mrs. Brawley. "You're leaving money on the table. We want fifty #$¢%& percent!"

Michael's face turned purple. "Grrrrrr, would you two please shut your fizzledripping flufferknuckle faces."

Then things got worse.

TV vans pulled up behind us.

TV helicopters hovered overhead.

There was even a TV guy on a scooter.

"We gotta run," Mom hollered out the car window to the Brawleys. "Hop in quick, Michael."

"You'll talk to your #@$%* ex-husband, right?" said Mr. Brawley.

"He shouldn't be the only £¢#&% getting rich off our kids," added Mrs. Brawley.

"I'll see what I can do," said Mom, then she muttered, "Not," as soon as Michael climbed into the car and slammed his door shut.

Mom floored the gas pedal. We raced up the street, but the news crews sped behind us. Except the guy on the scooter—he got knocked off his ride by the funnel cloud of garbage stirred up by all the helicopters.

Mom pulled into the drop-off lane at school.

So did the TV satellite trucks.

Principal Ferguson was standing at the front of the school, hiding behind two eighth-grade crossing guards who kept telling the pushy TV

reporters to "back off, dudes."

Principal Ferguson ushered Mom, Michael, and me into the building and then took us into his office and locked the door.

"I've been thinking," he said to Mom. "Maybe it would be best if Michael and David stayed home until this *Pottymouth and Stoopid* craze dies down. Maybe for a week. Make it a month. Heck, according to their IQ tests, they're both geniuses so they probably already know everything they would've been studying anyway."

Mom's jaw dropped. "They're *geniuses?*"

"Yes," said Principal Ferguson, nervously peeking through his venetian blinds at the mayhem out in the parking lot. "It's in their permanent records."

Mom grinned. "I knew it. My little Einsteins."

"That's a good idea," said Principal Ferguson. "Homeschool them for a while. Use those Baby Einstein videos."

"I can't. I have to go to work."

"She has three jobs," I added.

"I'm sorry, Mrs. Scungili. I'm sure you and your

husband can work something out."

And guess what? When the principal said that, Mom grinned again.

This time, the grin was extremely sly.

"You're right, Principal Ferguson. I'm certain we can. In fact, I know we will. Come on, David. Michael. We're heading home. I need to make a few phone calls."

"Ex-Dad?" I asked.

"Nope. I'm going to call a lawyer I know. *He* can call your ex-dad."

TONY SCUNGILI

David's "Ex-Dad"

I was sound asleep.

I'd just bought a top-of-the-line sleep-quotient adjustable bed. It's extremely comfy, and extremely expensive.

Anyway, I was sleeping and the phone starts ringing. I hate when it does that.

But when I saw the name in the Caller ID window, I knew I had to answer it. I'll be honest with you—the call kind of shook me up.

"I understand," I said into the phone. "I'm on it."

After a call like that, there was no way I could go back to sleep.

42

Hometown Heroes

Our awesome vacation from school didn't last very long—just two days.

On the afternoon of the second day, Principal Ferguson called Mom. "We'd like David and Michael to return to school."

Mom put her phone on speaker so I could hear what Principal Ferguson had to say, and she gave me another one of her sly grins.

"Really?" she said. "Have circumstances changed?"

"Everything has," said Principal Ferguson.

"Wow," said Mom coyly. "I wonder how that happened."

"I received a few very interesting phone calls," said Principal Ferguson.

"What a coincidence. I *made* a few very interesting phone calls. One was to a lawyer I know from the restaurant where I waitress. He likes our chicken noodle soup."

I'll call the Cartoon Factory in Chicago for you. Trust me, your ex will go down easy, just like this soup!

"Rest assured, ma'am," Principal Ferguson told Mom, "things are going to be very, very different here at school for Michael and David. For starters, we're moving them into our gifted and talented program."

Wow, I thought. *Gifted and talented* sounded a lot better than *Pottymouth and Stoopid.*

"We have some other surprises lined up too," said Principal Ferguson.

"Like what?" I blurted at the speakerphone.

"If I told you," said Principal Ferguson, "they wouldn't be surprises."

So the next morning, Michael and I went to school as usual. But the ride was anything but usual.

For starters, we weren't in Mom's clunker car. We were riding in an SUV with dark-tinted windows and a chauffeur behind the wheel. Two giant men had ushered us into the car.

"Gentlemen," the chauffeur had said to us in a thick Russian accent. "My name is Sergei. I will be your driver today. Your bodyguards are Olaf and Petro. They know many ways to relocate body parts."

Yep. We had bodyguards. And a police escort!

Fred Grabowski was standing in front of the school when our motorcade pulled up. "You guys deserve the escort," he gushed. "And you deserve *that* too!"

He pointed to a banner hanging on the front of the school: MICHAEL AND DAVID DAY!

"We're not Pottymouth and Stoopid any-more?" said Michael.

"Nope," said Fred. "Not today. Today you're our brand-new, internationally famous home-town heroes!"

43

Is This Real Life?

Michael and David Day started out extremely weird for us, like a pumped-up Opposite Day.

For one thing, the halls were mobbed with kids dressed up like characters from the show. Since the two main characters were Pottymouth and Stoopid, aka *us,* it was like Michael and I were walking through a funhouse filled with those wacky mirrors. Everywhere we looked, we saw chubby, skinny, tall, and short copies of ourselves.

Even weirder—we were being cheered and high-fived all around. It was like we were some kind of big heroes. There was even a cake. Two, actually, shaped and frosted to look like Pottymouth and Stoopid.

"You guys are the awesometastic-est!" cried Katherine Kelly, high-fiving us as we passed.

"You don't go to this school," I reminded her.

"I do now!" she said. "My parents moved to

this school district just so I could be closer to you two!"

Weird was becoming crazy.

Michael and I were the same kids we'd always been. We hadn't changed at all. (Okay, I was wearing a super-clean shirt, not just the first one out of the hamper that passed the sniff test.) The only thing different was everybody else's bizarre attitudes toward us!

Then crazy became creepy.

Teachers started acting nice to us too!

When we reached the school office, Principal Ferguson came out to fist-bump us. "Good morning, David. Michael. We have a very special day lined up for you two."

"Really?" I asked. "Are they serving Michael's chili-bacon-cheese corn dogs for lunch?"

"Maybe later. First, we're having an assembly."

"About what?" asked Michael.

"About you two."

"Grizzlesnorts!"

"It's true. It's all part of Michael and David Day."

That's when Kaya Kennecky rounded a corner to scowl at us. She was holding her cheerleader pom-poms so tightly they were vibrating even though she wasn't shaking them.

"And I get to lead all your cheers," she said through the tightest, fakest smile I have ever seen. "Isn't that special?"

"Yeah," said Michael doing his own version of Mom's sly grin. "Fripplegerkin special."

"Let's head to the gym!" said Principal Ferguson cheerily.

I shrugged. "Fine. Whatever."

As Michael and I strode up the corridor toward the gymnasium, we could hear the entire student body clapping to the beat as loudspeakers boomed the very familiar *Pottymouth & Stoopid* theme song.

When we climbed up the steps to the stage, we noticed someone very familiar sitting in one of the folding chairs with the other assorted grown-ups.

Ex-Dad.

44

Bullies Beware

Porter Malkiel, the big cheese from the Cartoon Factory, was sitting right next to my ex-dad.

Of course, I didn't know who he was until he stood up and shot out his arm to shake hands with us. He had a very strong grip for such a short guy. He wore black everything and had one of those triangle beards in the middle of his chin.

"Hi, guys," Mr. Malkiel said, like he wanted to slap us on the back. "We at the Cartoon Factory are *sooooo* glad your mother's lawyer called us to

let us know that you two were the true inspiration for the biggest hit in Cartoon Factory history."

"Is that why today's fricklebrickle Michael and David Day?" asked Michael. "So we don't sue your pants off?"

Mr. Malkiel laughed and snapped his fingers. "I like that." He whipped out his phone and started talking into it. "Note to self. New show. A court where the judge sentences you to twenty years without pants." He slipped his iPhone back into his sleek jeans. "Now here's how this assembly is going to work, gang. David, your father—"

"You mean my ex-father."

"Got it. Right. I'll introduce your ex-father, Tony Scungili. He'll yak a little."

"Really?" I asked. "What's he going to say?"

Mr. Malkiel gave us a wink. "Exactly what our lawyers told him to say. He's also signed documents granting you two a very generous percentage of his past, present, and future earnings on *P and S*."

"Awesometastic," said Michael.

"When he's done gabbing, you two get up and say a few words."

"Sludgepuggle," said Michael.

Mr. Malkiel arched an eyebrow and looked worried. "Well, maybe we'll just have *you* speak, David."

It was Michael's turn to shrug. "Whatever floats your boomboolie boat, Mr. Malkiel."

"Say a few words about what?" I'd never talked in front of a huge crowd like this, and I suddenly got the heebie-jeebies. "And what's with all the cameras?" I asked, noticing several film crews ringed around the stage. "Are we going to be on the local news again?"

"Nope," said the Cartoon Factory president. "We're shooting footage for an upcoming documentary."

"Cool," I said. "What's it about?"

"You two. The true story behind the making of America's favorite cartoon characters." He framed the air with his hands. *"Pottymouth and Stoopid: The Truth Behind the Laughs.* That's just the working title; I'll pay someone to come up with something better. Anyway, let's get going. You don't want to keep your fans waiting..."

The crowd was on its feet, stomping to the beat of the show's theme song, which seemed to be playing on some sort of endless loop.

Mr. Malkiel stepped up to the microphone.

"Hello, fellow knuckleheads and animation maniacs!" he said, and then he introduced himself.

The audience roared.

"You know," the head of the Cartoon Factory

continued, "when I was a kid, they used to tease me and call me Stubby because I was so vertically challenged. Okay, I was short. As you might imagine, I did not like being called Stubby. Or Stumpy. Or Oompa-Loompa. So that's why I was so glad when *Pottymouth and Stoopid* came along. Finally, someone was standing up for those of us who have been word-bullied our entire lives!"

Whhhhhhhhaaaaaaaaaat?

The show was *standing up* for us?

Huh. All along, I'd thought Ex-Dad and the Cartoon Factory were just making fun of us.

"Here to tell you more is the creator of *Pottymouth and Stoopid*. The very, shall we say, 'observant' Mr. Tony Scungili."

Ex-Dad was mopping his forehead with a doily from someone's grandmother's house (or a very expensive handkerchief; the kind fancy people in pirate movies always swish around).

Michael and I settled back in our chairs.

Seeing Ex-Dad sweat in front of his boss and five hundred middle-schoolers?

This was gonna be priceless.

45

How Do You Know Ex-Dad's Lying?

His Lips Are Moving

Ex-Dad shuffled nervously toward the microphone, fumbling with a stack of bright pink notecards in his hand.

"Um, hi," he said, leaning into the microphone because the stand had been lowered for President Stubby. "As those of you lucky enough to go to school with my son, David Scungili, and his best friend since forever, a kid I've known almost his entire life, Michael, uh, er...Michael..."

"It's Littlefield, sir," said Michael, rolling his eyes. "Sludgepuggle."

"That's right," Ex-Dad said quickly. "Michael Littlefield. He and David are super kids. I'm proud to know them both. And, yes, Michael and David were the inspiration for *Pottymouth and Stoopid*."

"No," shrieked Kaya from somewhere off in the distance. "It can't be true."

"It's true," shouted our second-biggest fan, Will Hunt. "Deal with it, sister!"

"It *is* true," said Ex-Dad. "You see, kids, I'm passionate about bringing the terrible issue of word-bullying to America's attention. It is something of a cause with me. I've always dreamed about doing a cartoon series that would show the world how some kids get unfairly labeled early in life. And those labels can be very hard to lose. They stick with you. Sort of like when you step in bubble gum. So that's why I created *Pottymouth and Stoopid*."

"Seriously?" shouted someone from the audience.

"You didn't just do it to be funny?" hollered another.

"Or for the moola?" yelled someone else.

"No," said Ex-Dad, shaking his head vigorously. "No, no, *no.* I was a man on a mission, hoping to erase our nation's plague of ugly name-calling!"

I also want to stamp out name-calling and labeling and all that other bad stuff the Cartoon Factory lawyers told me I should probably mention.

"But," said Ex-Dad when his armpits of his shirt were soaked through with sweat, "enough about me and my dreams. You came here today to celebrate and honor two of your own, Pottymouth and Stoopid. Er, I mean Michael and

David. One of whom, I am thrilled to call my son. The other I, uh, call Michael. Or Mike. But never Mikey. Because that would be, uh, labeling. I think. I'm not really sure..."

Still mumbling, Ex-Dad finally moved away from the microphone.

"Okay, David," whispered Mr. Malkiel. "You're on. Tell 'em everything."

"Everything?"

"The truth, the whole truth, and nothing but the truth."

"That could take a while, sir. I have like a whole novel's worth of stories to unload on these people."

"Take as long as you like, kiddo. We've booked the gym for the entire day. And who knows? When we put together your documentary, maybe we'll publish an illustrated book about you guys too!"

"Cool."

The stage was mine.

And this is the point where you came in, way back on page 1. Sorry for the loooong flashback.

"Okay," I said. "Everybody here already knows

us, right? We're Pottymouth and Stoopid, thanks to all of you. Those have been our names since you gave them to us, like, forever ago. We're the class clowns. No, wait. We're the class *jokes*."

I told them our real, true story.

And I told it our way.

As you know, I didn't leave anything out. The good, the bad, the ugly . . . and the even worse and the uglier.

I guess it was sort of "like father, like son"

(or, in my case, "like ex-dad, like son"), because I wanted to finish what he'd started talking about. I was also on a mission. But unlike my ex-dad, I wanted to tell the world how truly awful and hurtful and just plain mean labels can be.

Especially when they're completely wrong.

So my long life story you've been reading is the story I told. I talked about how it felt to be stuck with this name I couldn't shake. I tried to describe what it was like to be treated as if I were garbage by kids and teachers who hardly knew me. How angry and sad I felt all the time.

And how lucky I was to have friends like Michael and Anna.

When I was done, the audience clapped and cheered and gave us a standing ovation. Even Kaya Kennecky. (Of course, she's a cheerleader. Cheering is sort of her job.)

I have to tell you, I wish all that screaming and chanting and applause could've gone on forever. It was the first time that I'd felt happy to be in school.

Ever.

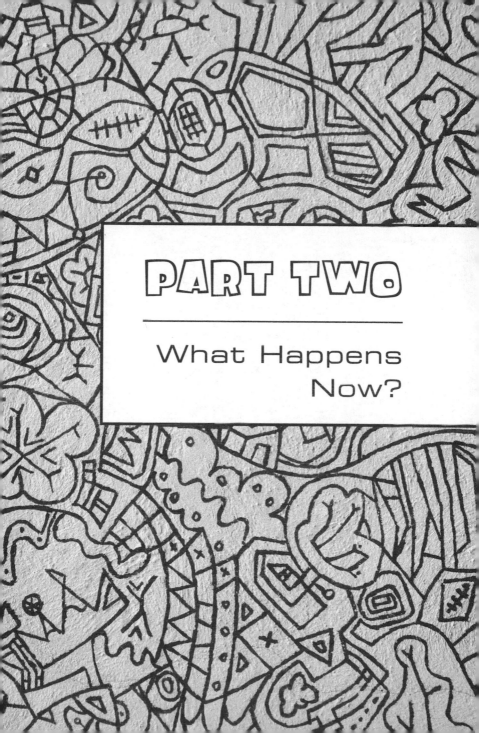

PART TWO

What Happens
Now?

46

Say Buh-Bye, Ex-Dad

So now we're all caught up.

After the mega-assembly, we lost our bodyguards and chauffeur. They needed to whisk el presidente, Mr. Porter Malkiel, off to his private jet. He was flying back to the Chicago headquarters of the Cartoon Factory.

"But let's keep in touch, you knuckleheads," he said to Michael and me. "I mean it." Then he turned his thumb and pinkie into a telephone, wiggled it alongside his head, and said, "I'll call you two later. Seriously."

I didn't expect to hear from him again. So far, the adults I'd met in the TV industry hadn't been all that reliable. Speaking of which...

Ex-Dad drove me, Michael, and Anna back to Mom's house in his fancy convertible.

It was an extremely tight squeeze.

It also made for a very interesting ride. Especially since I had never eaten mosquitoes or tasted gnats before.

Since we were riding in a car with the top down, everybody could see us, and we were easily spotted and then chased by the paparazzi. And the news helicopters. And a guy making pizza deliveries. (I think one of the TV reporters tailing us had ordered a pepperoni pie.)

Luckily, Mom had left the garage door open.

Ex-Dad zoomed right in. I hopped out and bopped the button to close the garage door.

"We made it." Anna sighed as she squeezed out of the backseat.

"Hicklesnicklepox," muttered Michael.

"Definitely," I said, agreeing with him.

"You boys are pretty popular now," said Ex-Dad, jabbing his finger at the closed garage door. "But fame has its price. The press? They'll hound you like rabid jackals. Especially if they find out you based a TV show on your son and his best friend and everybody thinks you're horrible for cashing in on their misery. And that you shouldn't make money making fun of poor, defenseless kids. How you're a terrible person, blah-blah-blah."

He realized we were staring at him and stopped.

It was kind of quiet. For about five seconds.

Then a whole mob of reporters started banging on the garage door.

"David?" shouted one, his voice muffled by the aluminum garage door. "What do you think about what your father did to you and your friends? Is he a horrible person? Is *Pottymouth and Stoopid* the meanest and most despicable, not to mention the most horrendous, thing any father has ever done to one of his own children in the history of fatherhood?"

"Okay," said Ex-Dad. "Gotta go."

He didn't even take his car. He just dashed out the garage's back door.

Then he stuck his head in again.

"Tell your mother not to get any ideas; I'm coming back for my convertible first thing tomorrow. Probably around three in the morning. That's when most reporters finally go to sleep. Be safe, boys and girl. Don't forget to watch *our* show. Tell all your friends."

And then he hightailed it across our backyard

and jumped over the neighbor's hedge, a couple of reporters at his heels.

Michael, Anna, and I kind of crept into the house. I peeked through the curtains in the living room.

The reporters had set up camp on our front lawn. Literally. A couple of them had brought along a portable grill so they could have a weenie roast.

Suddenly, the home phone rang. "Hello?" I asked.

"David, it's Porter Malkiel. President and chief executive officer of the Cartoon Factory. We did an assembly together today, remember?"

"Yes, sir."

"I'm calling from my private jet."

"Cool."

"I know. So, what are you and Michael doing tomorrow?"

"Um, going to school, I guess."

"Guess again. You're coming to Chicago! It's time our biggest stars finally visited the Cartoon Factory!"

Where the Magic Happens

So the very next day, Michael and I climbed into another limo and drove off to a strange private airfield to board a way cool corporate jet!

Talk about free snacks; this plane had everything, plus leather swivel seats!

Two hours later, we were in Chicago. Mom would've come with us but she had to work the early shift at the diner. Michael managed to get the Brawleys to okay the trip without giving them any details—he just asked them for permission to go while they were fighting.

Another limo was waiting to pick us up at O'Hare Airport. We were chauffeured downtown to the home of the Cartoon Factory studios!

Talk about awesometastic. This place was incredibly cool.

Dozens of computer geeks were tapping on keyboards while artists sketched on tablets. We saw two actors in headphones standing in a soundproof booth voicing the characters flitting across the big screen in front of them.

"Whoa," said Michael. "Those flufferknuckles are *us!*"

"Hey, welcome to the extremely hip and cool nerve center of the whole operation," said Mr. Malkiel as he came out of his glass box of an office. "This is where the magic happens, kiddos. This is where Pottymouth and Stoopid come to life."

Mr. Malkiel showed us around the production studio. We saw the storyboards where the episodes were roughed out. We saw the character artists, the guys who made sure Pottymouth and Stoopid looked the way they were supposed to in every frame. We met the painters and inkers who colored us in. (You have to figure they all aced "coloring inside the lines" in kindergarten.) Then we watched as the animators filmed an episode, one drawing at a time.

Okay, we watched them film only like five

seconds of the episode because that was all they could shoot in fifteen minutes. Animation takes a long, long time!

"It's great to actually meet you two," said one of the artists, slipping another drawing into the frame under the camera. "You guys are, like, the hippest kids who have ever lived! Seriously, the way you stand up to Principal Blerguson and that bratty Kara Kentucky is super-cool. And the way you always look out for each other, like true friends should. You're role models, dudes."

Michael and I had *never* been considered role models or anything close to hip and cool.

In fact, I don't think either one of us even knew what hip and cool was. But it didn't matter. All the hip and cool people in Chicago were really nice to us.

"Kids pick on you?" said this one lady who could draw all sorts of expressions and emotions for Pottymouth with a flick of her wrist—all she had to do was change the angle of his eyebrows. "Kids used to pick on me too. They called me Miss Artsy Fartsy in seventh grade and made fun of the doodles I did on my notebook covers. But guess what, guys? It gets better. *Way* better. The same people who make fun of you now will be working for you someday."

Everyone was so sweet to me and Michael, we figured we were going to have a sugar crash.

But you know what? We liked it.

No—we *looooved* it!

And then the nicest thing of all happened.

"So," said Mr. Malkiel, "how would you two like to write your own episode? Forget your ex-dad. Forget everything. Throw out all the rules. Write me a two-minute episode filled with as much truth and honesty as you put into your speech at the assembly and I'll find some place to run it. Can you do that, guys?"

"Fudging yes, we can," said Michael.

I just said, "Woo-hoo!"

This was going to be fun. Maybe even hip and cool!

48

Based on a True Story. Lots of Them

We sat in a room with a whole bunch of writers and started bouncing around ideas for our very own two-minute *Pottymouth & Stoopid* cartoon.

Turns out, each and every one of the writers in the room had been teased and bullied when they were our age. So in honor of our visit, they decided to put their middle-school nicknames on their name tags.

"I was the Stink," said a guy with glasses and short, spiky hair. "I swear I showered every day, so

I never understood why. But then, the cool kids who slapped these names on us weren't all that bright."

"But we were," said a girl in glasses. "That's why they called me Egghead when they weren't calling me Four-Eyes."

"I was Nerd Breath," said another writer, and, yes, he was wearing glasses too.

In fact, all the writers—including Spaz, Godzilla, Squirrel Girl, and Cheese Butt—wore big, thick glasses. Maybe they'd spent too much time geeking out in front of computer screens.

"I guess there have always been more licketerpicketer losers in middle school than whingeywhiney winners," said Michael.

All the writers nodded.

"At my school, we outnumbered the cool kids nine to one," said one of the girls in glasses (her bullied name was Wing Nut because her ears were so big). "Maybe we should've staged a revolution," she added with a laugh.

"Yes!" I said. "That's what this two-minute cartoon should be about. Pottymouth and Stoopid finally realize that they're not the only ones being picked on. That there's strength in numbers—"

"Yes!" said Michael. "A rattletrapple revolution!"

"We bring Anna Britannica back into the mix," said Egghead. "I *love* Anna Britannica."

"And we add in a new character named Wing Nut," said Wing Nut. "Her ears are so big, she can fly—like Dumbo!"

All the writers pitched character ideas.

"We build a super-team of incredibly smart and multitalented nerd warriors!"

"The Geek-Vengers!"

"Justice League of Nerdmerica?"

"We need a name that shows how being underdogs have made them all friends."

"Yeah!" I blurted out. "Because Michael and me? We're going to be friends forever!"

"Grandpa Johnny said so," added Michael.

"How about the Uncool Adventurers?"

"The Agents of Awkward?"

"I've got it," said Cheese Butt. "Pottymouth and Stoopid and the Picked-Last Posse!"

"That's it!" said Michael and I at the same time.

"But remember, you guys," Michael continued, "these supernerds need to do snipplesnapple, fliggilyflaggily funny stuff."

"Of course," said all the writers.

"Okay," said the writer wearing the name tag that said *Stink*. "We need our first supervillain."

"How about an evil bully named Tony Skunkjelly?" I said. "His power is making fun of all the other kids and giving them terrible names."

"He's extremely oily," said Egghead. "When he walks, we give his shoes a squishy, sloshy sound effect."

"Like he has wet poop in his shoes," said Michael.

"Ta-da!" said Squirrel Girl, who must have been an artist too. "Meet Mr. Skunkjelly."

What a coincidence.

Mr. Skunkjelly looked exactly like Ex-Dad, Tony Scungili.

49

Can Somebody Say *Spin-Off*?

The two-minute cartoon went exactly the way we wanted it to go.

It was kind of like a superhero comic book come to life! All about the incredibly smart and funny but uncool kids joining forces to stand up together against the big, mean (and somewhat smelly) bully.

It was about picked-on underdogs realizing they had the power to take back their schools and their lives.

It had a new theme song too!

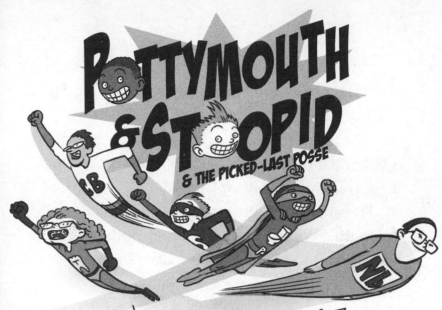

♫ PICK US LAST AND IT'S OK ♪
♪ 'CAUSE YOU'LL BE WORKING FOR US SOMEDAY! ♫

The opening scene showed the evil villain, the bully Tony Skunkjelly, picking on a kid he called Cheese Butt.

"Cheese Butt," he sneered. "That'll be your name for the rest of your life, punk! Why? Because I say so! And this is *my* school! Deal with it."

Cheese Butt whimpered a little. That's when Pottymouth and Stoopid swooped in.

"Yo," Pottymouth said to Skunkjelly. "Quit picking on the hicklesnicklepox kid!"

"But I must make fun of him." Skunkjelly cackled. "He smells weird and I can't let that slide. He is Cheese Butt! Now and forever!"

"Um, don't mean to be rude here," said Stoopid politely, fanning the air in front of his nose, "but have you smelled *yourself* lately?"

"Because we, unfortunately, have," said Pottymouth. "Whoa. How many dinkledorking bean burritos did you eat for lunch today?"

"Shut up, you losers!" cried Skunkjelly.

And that's where we introduced Pottymouth and Stoopid's new catchphrase.

"Uh-huh. Right back atcha!" sniggered Pottymouth and Stoopid.

"You would dare to stand up to me?" demanded Tony Skunkjelly.

"Uh, yeah," said Stoopid. "I think there's more of us than you."

"One, two, three!" counted Cheese Butt. "Yup, I'm pretty sure three is more than one."

A girl with braces barged into the scene. "Make that four, CB! I'm Tinsel Teeth!"

"Five!" said another supernerd, bursting into

the frame. "Whoa. Who cut the cheese?"

"Silence!" yelled Skunkjelly. "You morons are nothing but lousy lamebrains!"

And then all the cartoon kids with nicknames pointed at Skunkjelly and said, chuckling, "Uh-huh. Right back atcha!"

It took all day for us to bang out the script and storyboard the idea, even though the final cartoon would be only two minutes long. The Cartoon Factory artists took a week to produce it. When they were finally finished, the two-minute clip ran only on their website.

But we were extremely proud of it. We figured it might give all the Pottymouths, Stoopids, Nerd Breaths, Wing Nuts, and Cheese Butts out there a little hope that things *can* get better. Especially if everyone looks out for one another.

Anyway, that two-minute clip of *Pottymouth & Stoopid and the Picked-Last Posse* on the Cartoon Factory website was a huge hit. Actually, it was ginormous. Maybe even bigger than the original *Pottymouth & Stoopid.*

In no time, the clip went viral. People kept e-mailing and texting and tweeting the link. A week later, *The Picked-Last Posse* became a brand-new spin-off show on the Cartoon Factory channel!

They still ran the original *Pottymouth & Stoopid* show but with some major changes because, thanks to Mr. Malkiel, both shows now had two new executive producers.

Yeah. Me and Michael! (We could do it only part-time because we still had to go to school. It's a law or something.)

As for Ex-Dad?

He still has a job writing scripts.

Only now he works for *us*.

Hot Dogs Taste Better in New York City

As awesome as it was to be executive producers of *Pottymouth & Stoopid,* you know what the best part was?

We got paid to do it!

We received a pretty hefty chunk of change every week. In fact, we earned enough to pay for our college educations while making it possible for Mom to quit two of her three jobs and buy a new, nonclunker car.

Michael gave his foster parents a pile of cash

too—but he told them they had to use some of it to go to anger-management classes.

In November, our school scheduled a class trip to New York City, and, for the first time since my grade started going on field trips, Michael and I were able to go. We could finally afford to pay for the bus tickets and the hotel and all the cool stuff we were going to do, like catch a Broadway show and look at the holiday windows in all the big department stores.

"Why take the bus?" said Mr. Malkiel when we had our weekly conference call to kick around new ideas for *Pottymouth & Stoopid* and the spin-off. "We'll send the corporate jet to pick you boys up and drop you off in the Big Apple. It's the least we can do for the stars of the Cartoon Factory's *two* biggest shows!"

"Thanks, but we don't mind taking the bofforrific bus," Michael told him.

"We're kind of looking forward to hanging with our peeps," I added.

"Your peeps?"

"Yeah. Anna Brittoni, Fred Grabowski, Will Hunt, Katherine Kelly, a guy they call Norkface, a girl who's been called Snotboogers since third grade..."

Mr. Malkiel chuckled into the phone. "Just like in *The Picked-Last Posse,* huh? Oh, by the way, be prepared for a couple of big surprises when you get to the Big Apple."

"What kind of surprises?" I asked.

"Hey, it's New York. Anything's possible in that crazy town! Catch you later. I have to talk to the flufferknuckles down in the legal department."

Early the next morning, a crisp, fall Wednesday, we climbed into the chartered bus and took off for New York City with our new friends. Yes, the cool kids sat in the back and tried to annoy us with spitballs and paper-clip projectiles.

But then, at exactly the same time, we all turned around and stared at them, totally silently.

The cool kids could count. There were fifty of us. Twelve of them.

The rest of the ride was kind of fun. When Kaya Kennecky tried to start a sing-along of "The Wheels on the Bus," we all turned around and stared her down again.

New York City was even better. We did all the important cultural stuff: We visited Nike Town, had our picture taken with Spider-Man in Times Square, and chowed down as many of Nathan's Famous hot dogs as we could stomach in honor of Takeru Kobayashi, the famous Japanese competitive eater (that's my kind of sport). Kobayashi has won a bunch of Guinness World Records for eating, among other things, hot dogs (he gobbled down sixty-nine in ten minutes), meatballs, Twinkies, hamburgers, pizza, and pasta. I'm guessing that when he was in middle school, all the kids called him Garbage Gullet.

Well, guess who's laughing and burping in their faces now? Takeru Kobayashi is definitely a *Pottymouth & Stoopid* kind of guy.

Heck, everybody is.

Even Kaya Kennecky.

"I'm different too," she told us when she posed for her Times Square photo with Elmo instead of Spidey. "For instance, once, when I was in second grade, this really mean fifth-grade girl made fun of my nail-polish color!"

Okay. It was a start.

What is it that makes New York City so supercool? It's this: Everybody you see on the street is so different, it's easy for all of them to fit in.

51

Thanks Giving

Our second day in New York wasn't just another ordinary Thursday—it was Thanksgiving.

We all got up before dawn so we could go shiver on the sidewalk in front of our hotel and watch the truly amazing Macy's Thanksgiving Day Parade pass by.

We saw marching bands, roller-skating clowns, weeble-wobbly big-headed Pilgrims, a giant motorized turkey, and lots of jumbo-size-cartoon balloons.

Including two floating giants who looked incredibly familiar.

"Whoa!" Michael and I shouted at the same time. All around us, our friends squealed.

"You think this is what Mr. Malkiel meant when he told us to be prepared for a couple of *big* surprises?" I asked.

"Hicklesnicklepox, yes!" said Michael. "Surprises don't come much bigger than those two!"

One of the guys holding the strings to the Stoopid balloon saw me in the crowd.

"Hey," he cried out. "You look just like my balloon!"

"No," I said. "Your balloon looks just like me!"

And do you know what he said in reply? "Uh-huh. Right back atcha!"

When Pottymouth floated past, the whole crowd started chanting, "*Fluf*-fer-*knuck*-le! *Fluf*-fer-*knuck*-le!"

Later, after Santa had ho-ho-hoed his way past our sidewalk viewing spot and the parade was over, our class headed uptown to a restaurant so everybody could eat some Thanksgiving turkey. Well, everybody except Anna and a few others. They were going to order the Tofurkey. Don't ask.

On our way to the restaurant, we passed all sorts of kids wearing *Pottymouth & Stoopid* sweatshirts or carrying miniature versions of our helium balloons.

Four goofy-looking guys were walking south while we were walking north.

They saw Michael and me. They grinned and waved. Yeah, they were doofuses just like us.

And then one of them said, "Hey, David! Hey, Michael! Thanks for everything!"

It was kind of amazing. The best Thanksgiving

of my life and I hadn't even scooped the marsh-mallow goop off the candied yams with my finger yet.

We were David and Michael.

Finally.

But being Pottymouth and Stoopid had helped a whole bunch of other kids be who they really were too.

So maybe all the bad stuff we had to go through was sort of worth it.

There's something my mom once said that stuck with me (like a bad nickname, but way nicer): You can't see the stars shine until it gets really, really dark.

For Michael and me, aka ex-Pottymouth and ex-Stoopid?

It was our turn to shine.

P.S.

Oh, that book the Cartoon Factory said they might make about us?

You just read it!

HI, FRIEND.

My name is Max Einstein, and
I'm not your typical kid genius.
I've been recruited by the mysterious
Change Makers organization
for a super-secret mission:
to help solve the world's toughest
problems using science.
We're going to
change the world—
if the evil Corporation
doesn't get to us first...

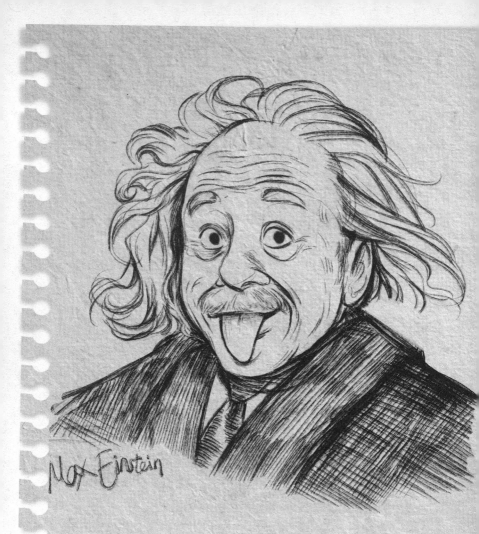

Max Einstein

Imagination is more
important than knowledge.
    - Albert Einstein

1

The stench of horse manure woke Max Einstein with a jolt.

"Of course!"

Even though she was shivering, she threw off her blanket and hopped out of bed. Actually, it wasn't really a bed. More like a lumpy, water-stained mattress with frayed seams. But that didn't matter. Ideas could come wherever they wanted.

She raced down the dark hall. The floorboards—bare planks laid across rough beams—creaked and wobbled with every step. Her red hair, of course, was a bouncing tangle of wild curls. It was always a bouncing tangle of wild curls.

Max rapped her knuckles on a lopsided door hanging off rusty hinges.

"Mr. Kennedy?" She knocked again. "Mr. Kennedy?"

"What the…" came a sleepy mumble. "Max? Are you okay?"

Max took that question as permission to enter Mr. Kennedy's apartment. She practically burst through his wonky door.

"I'm fine, Mr. Kennedy. In fact, I'm better than fine! I've got something great here! At least I think it's something great. Anyway, it's really, really cool. This idea could change everything. It could save our world. It's what Mr. Albert Einstein would've called an 'aha' moment."

"Maxine?"

"Yes, Mr. Kennedy?"

"It's six o'clock in the morning, girl."

"Is it? Sorry about the inconvenient hour. But you never know when a brainstorm will strike, do you?"

"No. Not with *you,* anyway…"

Max was wearing a floppy trench coat over her shabby sweater. Lately, she'd been sleeping in the sweater under a scratchy horse blanket because her so-called bedroom was, just like Mr. Kennedy's, extremely cold.

The tall and sturdy black man, his hair flecked with patches of white, creaked out of bed and rubbed some of the sleep out of his eyes. He slid his bare feet into shoes he had fashioned out of cardboard and old newspapers.

"Hang on," he said. "Need to put on my bedroom slippers here…"

"Because the floor's so cold," said Max.

"Huh?"

"You needed to improvise those bedroom slippers because the floor's cold every morning. Correct?"

"Maxine—we're sleeping, uninvited, above a horse stable. Of course the floors are cold. And, in case you haven't noticed, the place doesn't smell so good, either."

Max, Mr. Kennedy, and about a half-dozen other homeless people were what New York City called "squatters." That meant they were living rent-free in the vacant floors above a horse stable. The first two floors of the building housed a parking garage for Central Park carriages and stalls for the horses that pulled them. The top three floors? As far as the owner of the building knew, they were vacant.

"Winter is coming, Mr. Kennedy. We have no central heating system."

"Nope. We sure don't. You know why? Because we don't pay rent, Max!"

"Be that as it may, in the coming weeks, these floors will only become colder. Soon, we could all freeze to death. Even if we were to board up all the windows—"

"That's not gonna happen," said Mr. Kennedy. "We

3

need the ventilation. All that horse manure downstairs, stinking up the place…"

"Exactly! That's precisely what I wanted to talk to you about. That's my big idea. *Horse manure!*"

2

"It's simple, really, Mr. Kennedy," said Max, moving to the cracked plaster wall and finding a patch that wasn't covered with graffiti.

She pulled a thick stub of chalk out her baggy sweater pocket and started sketching on the wall, turning it into her blackboard.

"Please hear me out, sir. Try to see what I see."

Max, who enjoyed drawing in a beat-up sketchbook she rescued from a Dumpster, chalked in a lump of circles radiating stink marks. She labeled it "manure/biofuel."

"To stay warm this winter, all we have to do is arrange a meeting with Mr. Sammy Monk."

"The owner of this building?" said Mr. Kennedy,

skeptically. "The landlord who doesn't even know we're here? *That* Mr. Sammy Monk?"

"Yes, sir," said Max, totally engrossed in the diagram she was drafting on the wall. "We need to convince him to let us have all of his horse manure."

Mr. Kennedy stood up. "All of his manure? Now why on earth would we want that, Max? It's manure!"

"Well, once we have access to the manure, I will design and engineer a green gas mill for the upstairs apartments."

"A green what mill?"

"Gas, sir. We can rig up an anaerobic digester that will turn the horse manure into biogas, which we can then combust to generate electricity and heat."

"You want to burn horse manure gas?"

"Exactly! Anaerobic digestion is a series of biological processes in which microorganisms break down biodegradable material, such as horse manure, in the absence of oxygen, which is what 'anaerobic' means. That's the solution to our heating and power problems."

"You sure you're just twelve years old?"

"Yes. As far as I know."

Mr. Kennedy gave Max a look that she, unfortunately, was used to seeing. The look said she was crazy. Nuts. Off her rocker. But Max never let "the look" upset her. It was like Albert Einstein said, "Great spirits have always encountered violent opposition from mediocre minds."

Not that Mr. Kennedy had a mediocre mind. Max just wasn't doing a good enough job explaining her bold new breakthrough idea. Sometimes, the ideas came into her head so fast they came out of her mouth in a mumbled jumble.

"All we need, Mr. Kennedy, is an airtight container— something between the size of an oil drum and a tanker truck." She sketched a boxy cube fenced in by a pen of steel posts. "Heavy plastic would be best, of course. And it would be good if it had a cage of galvanized iron bars surrounding it. Then we just have to measure and cut three different pipes—one for feeding in the manure, one for the gas outlet, and one for displaced liquid fertilizer. We would insert these conduits into the tank through a universal seal, hook up the appropriate plumbing, and we'd be good to go."

Mr. Kennedy stroked his stubbly chin and admired Max's detailed design of the device sketched on the flaking wall.

"A brilliant idea, Max," he said. "Like always."

Max allowed herself a small, proud smile.

"Thank you, Mr. Kennedy."

"Slight problem."

"What's that, sir?"

"Well, that container there. The cube. That's what? Ten feet by ten feet by ten feet?"

"About."

"And you say you need a cage of bars around it. You also mentioned three pipes. And plumbing. Then I figure you're going to need a furnace to burn the horse manure gas, turn it into heat."

Max nodded. "And a generator. To spin our own electricity."

"Right. Won't that cost a whole lot of money?"

Max lowered her chalk. "I suppose so."

"And have you ever noticed the one thing most people squatting in this building don't have?"

Max pursed her lips. "Money?"

"Uhm-hmm. Exactly."

Max tucked the stubby chalk back into her sweater pocket and dusted off her pale, cold hands.

"Point taken, Mr. Kennedy. As usual, I need to be more practical. I'll get back to you with a better plan. I'll get back to you before winter comes."

"Great. But, Max?"

"Yes, sir?"

Mr. Kennedy climbed back into his lumpy bed and pulled up the blanket.

"Just don't get back to me before seven o'clock, okay?"

3

Max glanced at her watch.

It was only 6:17 a.m. She, unlike Mr. Kennedy, was an early riser. Always had been, probably always would be. The morning, especially that quiet space between dreaming and total wakefulness, was when most of her massive ideas floated through her drowsy brain. The ideas helped tamp down the sadness that could come in those same quiet times. A sadness that all orphans probably shared. Made more intense because Max had no idea who either of her parents were.

Max creaked her way back up the hall to her room as quietly as she could. She could hear Mr. Kennedy already snoring behind her.

Max had decorated her own sleeping space in the stables building the same way she had decorated all the rooms she had ever temporarily lived in: by propping open her battered old suitcase on its side to turn it into a display case for all things Albert Einstein. Books by and about the famous scientist were lined along the bottom like a bookshelf. Both lids were filled with her collection of Einstein photographs and quotes. She even had an Einstein bobblehead doll she'd found, once upon a time, in a museum store dumpster. She used it as a bookend.

Max couldn't remember where the suitcase came from. She'd just always had it. It was older than her rumpled knit sweater, and that thing was an antique.

The oldest photograph in her collection, the one that someone other than Max (she didn't know who) had pasted inside the suitcase lid so long ago that its edges were curling, showed the great professor lost in thought. He had a bushy mustache and long, unkempt hair. His hands were clasped together, almost as if in prayer. His eyes were gazing up toward infinity.

That photograph was Max's oldest memory. And since she never knew her own parents, at an early age, Max found herself talking to the kind, grandfatherly man at bedtime. He was a very good listener. She became curious as to who the mystery man might be, and that's how her lifelong infatuation with all things Einstein began. Like how he was born in Germany but had to leave his home before the Second World War. And how he was so busy thinking of big, amazing ideas, he sometimes forgot

to pay attention to his job at the patent office. They had a lot in common.

Next to the photograph was Max's absolute favorite Einstein quote: "Imagination is more important than knowledge."

"Unless, of course, you don't have the money to make the things you dream up come true," Max muttered.

Mr. Kennedy was right.

She couldn't afford to build her green gas mill. And she couldn't ask Mr. Sammy Monk for his horse manure or anything else because Mr. Sammy Monk couldn't know anybody was living in the abandoned floors of his horse stable. She'd just have to imagine a different solution to the squatters' heating dilemma. One that didn't cost a dime and could be created out of someone else's discarded scraps.

Max turned to her computer, which she had built herself from found parts. It was amazing what some people in New York City tossed to the curb on garbage pickup days. Max had been able to solder together (with a perfectly good soldering iron someone had thrown out) enough discarded circuit boards, unwanted wiring, abandoned processors, rejected keyboards, and one slightly blemished retina screen from a cast-off MacBook Pro to create a machine that whirred even faster than her mind.

She also had free wi-fi, thanks to the Link NYC public hot spot system. She could even recharge her computer's batteries (discovered abandoned behind one of the city's glossy Apple stores) at the kiosk just down the block from the stables. (Reliable wi-fi was one of the main reasons Max had selected her current accommodations. Easy access to a top-flight school was the other.)

Max clicked open a browser and went back to the internet page she had bookmarked the night before.

It was a nightmarish news report about children as young as seven "working in perilous conditions in the Democratic Republic of the Congo to mine cobalt that ends up in smartphones, cars, and computers sold to millions across the world." The children, as many as forty thousand, were being paid one dollar a day to do backbreaking work. They were also helping make a shadowy international business consortium called the Corp very, very, *very* rich.

The story broke Max's heart.

Because Max's heart, like her hero Dr. Einstein's, was huge.

Check out

Available now!

ABOUT THE AUTHORS

James Patterson received the Literarian Award for Outstanding Service to the American Literary Community from the National Book Foundation. He holds the Guinness World Record for the most #1 *New York Times* bestsellers, including *Middle School, I Funny,* and *Jacky Ha-Ha,* and his books have sold more than 385 million copies worldwide. A tireless champion of the power of books and reading, Patterson created a children's book imprint, JIMMY Patterson, whose mission is simple: "We want every kid who finishes a JIMMY Book to say, 'PLEASE GIVE ME ANOTHER BOOK.'" He has donated more than one million books to students and soldiers and funds over four hundred Teacher Education Scholarships at twenty-four colleges and universities. He has also donated millions of dollars to independent bookstores and school libraries. Patterson invests proceeds from the sales of JIMMY Patterson Books in pro-reading initiatives.

Chris Grabenstein is a *New York Times* bestselling author who has collaborated with James Patterson on the I Funny, Max Einstein, Jacky Ha-Ha, Treasure Hunters, and House of Robots series, as well as *Word of Mouse, Katt vs. Dogg, Pottymouth and Stoopid, Laugh Out Loud,* and *Daniel X: Armageddon.* He lives in New York City.

Stephen Gilpin lives and works in a cave just north of Hiawatha, Kansas, with his wife, Angie, their kids, and an infestation of dogs.